# THE
# BITTER
# HEIR
## AND THE
# BEAUTY

## ELLIE HALL

# Hogwash Holler

hôg′wôsh / hol·ler
noun/verb

1. Worthless, false, or ridiculous speech or writing; nonsense
2. To gripe or complain at a high volume
3. A small town that's a little rough around the edges but has a big heart and maybe some secrets too

# THE PEST DIGEST

## GARDENING & GOSSIP IN HOGWASH HOLLER

BRINGING YOU LOCAL NEWS, DRAMA, AND MORE

The Lazy Gator Grill

The grand opening of the refurbished Penny Gamble Soda Fountain and the Coffee Loft franchise aren't the only recent newsworthy events in Hogwash Holler. *Editorial Note: if anyone has information on the reports of vaporized space aliens landing in Daley's field, please email MEH@ThePestDigest.com*

Rumor has it the ownership of the town has been transferred. You might say we're under new management. Could it be our future mayor? *Editorial Note: Concerned citizens, reach out if you contest our last election when Chick Jagger was voted in. He is an angry bird who abandoned his flock. He'll do the same to the good people of Hogwash!)*

## THE WEEKLY STATUS UPDATE BY Y M.E.H.

We hear Hogwash's new landlord is a firefighter from out west. Hot stuff coming through! But will this city slicker stick around? Perhaps he'll find treasure—not the scavenger hunt kind—but the heart of this town. Or will he exit through the revolving door at the end of Main Street? *Editorial Note: If anyone has photographs of our latest resident that are suitable for a calendar, submit them at your earliest convenience.*

Congratulations to our very own Honey Hamilton. She recently added a new member to her family. Due to speculation about the source of the newborn, an opinion poll reports residents consistently seeing her for the last nine months and concluded they never saw a bump, meaning she wasn't pregnant. However, some suggest she did have a food baby on Independence Day after a visit to the burrito truck. *Editorial Note: seeking a tracking status update for the delivery of this infant. Reliable sources only.*

**-HOGWASH PEST #1**

P.S. Be sure to flip the page for all-natural mealy bug solutions and formulations.

# Chapter 1

## *Hashtag Mombie Life*

Sleep is an underrated staple in life until you're running on a deficit. Forget zombie. I'm officially a mombie.

I'm only hoping to get back to Hogwash Holler before—a deep rumble comes from the backseat. Ironic that we're driving past Pouppeville.

Hoping a distraction will thwart the impending situation, I start singing, "Rain, rain go away, come again another ..."

As the windshield wipers swipe the glass at a furious pace, reminding me to slow down, Leonie laughs...then toots again.

*Please don't let it turn into a crampy cry.*

I named the baby Leonie because she roars like a lion cub. Also, it was my great-grandmother's name. While my mother was otherwise occupied, my grandmother bore the brunt of making sure I didn't get into too much trouble before she passed away.

Aside from previous involvement with *Les Trois Tasses*, my old partner in teenage delinquency and I are now on the right side of the law.

Eager to get home to take care of Leonie's "business," I resist the temptation to put the pedal to the metal.

On account of me not turning in Jesse on more than one occasion, he typically won't pull me over for having a lapsed registration or going a few miles over the speed limit, but I'm not in my car today. To be fair, I usually try to stick to the rules of the road during operating hours out of respect for our Deputy Sheriff.

I try another nursery rhyme drawn from the depths of my memory. "Row, row, row your boat gently down the ..."

Leonie coos and burbles in the backseat, making baby noises.

*Crisis averted, I hope.*

I yawn while trying to draw a deep breath. This morning was intense and not because I had to change out of my one nice outfit because Leonie spit up on me before we left on our errand. Nor was it because Minou streaked through the house with a mouse—again. I'm afraid she's found herself a tomcat and is trying to impress him, or she doesn't like how the new resident in the Hamilton household interferes with her cat naps.

Never mind it being a long morning, it's been a long couple of months.

I'm officially a mom. I just signed the documents and every-thing—though I know well enough that ink on a piece of paper doesn't make a mother. I'm still learning what does since mine held a loose definition of motherhood and the law.

Leonie gets the kind of quiet that comes before a storm.

*Uh oh. Crisis back on?*

I try another song from the depths of my memory. "Hick-ory, dickory, dock ..."

She lets out a shriek.

I've been told I have pageant-worthy beauty, but my tone-deaf singing is probably more alarming than soothing or entertaining to a baby.

But it's past her naptime. I'm out of clean diapers, and hers is going to be dirty at any moment. I'm new at this but can read the signs ... and smells.

"We're almost there, sweet girl," I say in my normal voice.

She lets out a happy sound, and I hear her little feet kicking the back of the seat. I had the option to borrow Bruce Landry's ancient Buick Century or Missy Groveland's Corolla and went with the latter because it seemed the more practical choice, given my situation. Better on fuel, too.

For your information, the word *borrow* doesn't have air quotes around it. I am not Lisette "Luckie" Hamilton, thank you very much. I'll refill the gas tank and Missy will get all-she-can-eat pancakes on me at the Laughing Gator Grille this week.

As I pull onto Metairie Road, I've never been so relieved to be back in Hogwash Holler. The gas will have to wait. Er, for the car. From the odor filtering from the back seat, the damage is done. But Baby Girl will only be in a dirty diaper a moment longer because we're almost to the mobile home park.

Like a pit crew at a speedway, I have the baby in the house, on the changing table, and out of the soiled situation in less than fifteen seconds. It wouldn't fly for NASCAR, but it works for Leonie because her squished-up face and the fierce cry coming from her lips dissolve into a smile.

And she gets tickles and raspberries and nose nuzzles from me.

"Who's my sweet girl who was an angel at the lawyer's office? Who impressed everyone with her absolute cuteness? Who has a clean diaper and is about to get lunch and a nap?"

I didn't ask for this role. Didn't sign up. No invitation came in the mail. I certainly didn't RSVP, but here I am, on the receiving end of a full-fledged Leonie smile, and it's the greatest gift in the world.

I never knew a love so full could exist—certainly not between a baby that was left on my doorstep and me. But I wouldn't trade any of it for all the treasure in the world. Not even the sleepless nights, the diaper change sprint, or the bewildering look she sometimes gives me.

It's like we're both still trying to figure each other out and how we got here. But if I can do one thing right in my life, it's being the best mother possible for this little girl.

I could stay here all day gazing into her eyes, but I don't trust Molly at the Grille for another moment and this little peach needs a nap.

Back in the car, I drop Leonie off with Lexi and JQ and then return the Corolla to Missy. Crossing the street to avoid Mrs. Halfpenny's daily diatribe about how this town has gone to the dogs—never mind that hers is battery-operated—I all but run to the restaurant.

After this morning, I could really go for a lollipop. It became a habit after I quit smoking. This was B.B. as in *Before Baby* over ten years ago. I'd picked up the habit for three months after Cory died. But then quit and lollipops became my vice. I like all kinds—the gourmet, round ones, the cheap flat ones, and even the giant colorful ones.

Entering through the Grille's back door, I duck into the office and check my private stash in the bottom drawer of the desk. Fresh out of 'pops ... and looking like a madwoman in the speckled mirror by the door. Smoothing my hair and applying a fresh coat of red lipstick, the race to the end of the day begins in three, two, one.

Tying on my apron and stepping through the double-swinging wooden doors to the dining room, I find Molly leaning on the counter.

Mr. Soto sits at the other end, drinking his daily milkshake. It's Friday, which means he splurges on chocolate.

I stare at Molly and snap my fingers. "At attention."

She quickly straightens and all but salutes me. What can I say? I run a tight ship.

"Betsy might let you get away with *leaning* over at the Hogwash Hairwash & Style, but there's always something to do here while you're on the clock."

"Does that mean you're paying me?" Molly's Cajun accent used to be nearly as thick as mine, but lately, she's been using a more neutral tone like a news anchor.

I clear my throat. "I'm paying you with pancakes. That was the agreement."

I'm lucky I have enough money to keep the lights on.

"Pancakes with extra whipped cream?" Molly asks.

"Fine."

Roxanne Lagniappe, Molly's cohort, sits on the spinning stool on the other side of the counter.

"Are you going to order anything?" I ask.

It's not that she's keeping a spot from a paying customer, but if she's going to take up space, she may as well contribute.

"Can I see a menu?" she asks.

It hasn't changed in twenty years, so I imagine she has it memorized along with everyone else in town, but I slide one in front of her all the same. The laminate pulled away and water seeped inside, making the alligator on the logo look drunk.

"Can I get an apron next time?" Molly asks, eyeing mine, embroidered with my name in yellow thread.

"Who said there'll be a next time?" I ask while wiping down the counter.

"I know where you went today."

Of course she does.

Hogwash Holler Fact Number One: There are no

secrets. What you think you're keeping to yourself is always public knowledge. Perhaps there's something in the water. Or we all talk in our sleep. Could be a truth serum in the coffee. Then again, until recently, I was the only game in town who served the stuff. A Coffee Loft opened down the street and they likely have a proprietary formulation sans truth serum.

The source and purveyor of our town's gossip is none other than Molly Hazelwood. We went to high school together, and she knows everything, usually even before the people involved do. She moonlights as a receptionist at the hair salon a couple of days a week—a prime location for gathering juicy gossip, second to this very counter.

It's hard not to keep my ears open, but my mouth remains shut. I've been on the wrong side of gossip enough in my life to know better than to blab.

She says, "As a result of your meeting earlier, you'll probably need help around here from time to time."

This is likely true. I'm new to the single mom gig and, as it is, I stitch together trustworthy childcare with a very thin piece of thread. I don't trust Leonie in Molly's care, but can I depend on her to keep my business from burning down? That almost happened once, well, before I took ownership.

"I'll let you know," I reply.

Roxanne passes me the menu, apparently having satisfied her curiosity that nothing has changed. "I'll just take a coffee with cream and sugar."

Molly whispers, "Coffee Loft has better coffee."

I elbow her. "You're not supposed to say that."

"But it's true."

"Since when do you care about the truth?"

"It's the guiding principle for the Pest Digest."

I grunt. "Emphasis on *pest*."

Ignoring my comment, yet embodying it, she asks, "What do you think about adding cream brool to the menu?"

"What is cream brool?" I ask while fetching Mr. Soto his post-milkshake ice water. He says the dairy makes him congested, yet he continues to come back for more.

"Cream brool. The dessert," Molly says.

Frowning, I shake my head. "Never heard of it."

Roxanne shrugs. A fan of sweets, Mr. Soto leans in, listening intently.

Face scrunched up like we're a bunch of fools, Molly says, "Don't be silly. Of course you've heard of it. It's a pudding or custard or something like that. The top gets burned with a torch, like in those fancy French restaurants in New Orleans."

"This isn't a fancy French restaurant."

"But you're French."

"Hardly." I yawn. I pour myself a sweet tea and drizzle in some honey.

"I had that once," Roxanne says, snapping her gum.

"Cream brool, new menu item," Molly says with a flourish.

Brow crinkling as if I'm translating the Lost Southern Sea Scroll, I ask, "Do you mean crème brûlée?"

She shakes her head. "No, it's brool."

"That doesn't sound too appetizing." Roxanne wrinkles her nose.

The real reason I haven't changed the menu this decade is because I cannot afford it. In fact, I'm the one who started the rumor that the Pappadeaux Seafood Fondeux gave an out-of-towner food poisoning. Both are big fibs, but fancy cheese prices went up and they don't fit in my wholesale order budget, so I had to cleverly eighty-six it.

I shoo Molly toward the customer side of the counter. "Do you want your pancakes now?"

*Please say later.*

"I'll take a cream brool."

I shake my head.

Roxanne gets to her feet, coffee in hand. She and an accomplice stole the giant rotating root beer mug from the Tickle property not long ago. In much the same way that I don't trust Molly with information, I keep a careful eye on Roxanne's sticky fingers.

"The coffee mugs stay here."

Molly, halfway to the door, doubles back. "Speaking of, did you hear about JQ and Lexi?"

I've certainly heard things. Will I repeat them? No.

Molly waggles her eyebrows. "The key wasn't there."

Roxanne says, "What makes you think there's a key?"

"A key to what?" I ask mostly to annoy Molly, even though supposedly they found something at the Penny Gamble during their recent renovations.

Molly says, "To the treasure chest."

I roll my eyes.

She crosses her arms in front of her chest, picking up a long-standing debate among residents of Hogwash Holler. Some insist Hogan Tickle left behind clues that lead to X-marks the spot booty buried in a box in the ground. Others, like myself, are adamantly certain it does not exist.

Molly says, "There is a treasure chest."

"No, there's not," I reply.

"How can you be so sure?"

My mother would've found it. Luckie gambled, swindled, and did whatever she could to dishonestly earn money. If there was a bounty to be had, I wouldn't have been taught to shoplift at the age of five.

"Do you think the new guy will find it?" Roxanne asks with a tremor in her voice, as if nervous about the competition.

"What new guy?" I ask because this is news to me.

Molly starts, "Speaking of fires ..."

Eyes widening, I dash toward the kitchen.

She calls after me, "Not in there."

Extinguisher in hand, I check to be sure. Hand on my hip, I turn back to Molly. "Do not scare me like that."

If this place goes up in flames, I won't collect the insurance money on principle—because everyone will think I did it by association. Yes, my mother is in jail because of arson, among other things.

"I hear he's a firefighter." Molly waggles her eyebrows.

"Who is *he* and if that's the case, what is he doing here?" We have a volunteer fire department.

"Here?" Molly whirls around as if excited that he just walked in.

Nope. It's still just the three of us and Mr. Soto.

Eyes big, I blink, concerned that I'm surrounded by fools. "I mean in Hogwash."

"To save people and houses, obviously." Molly smiles like there's more to the story.

Does this town look like it needs saving? Yes.

Do I? Some days are more challenging than others.

Roxanne looks around, then at a whisper, she says, "By houses, Molly means rumor has it he inherited the Tickle Chateau."

Molly adds, "And that's not all."

Still not sure who this mysterious *he* is, despite my no-gossip policy, my eyebrows lift in question.

"I hear he's hot." Molly fans herself.

"Handsome in flannel," Roxanne adds.

Molly trills, "The perfect fall pair."

"It may be October, but it's almost seventy-five degrees out."

"Sixty-eight," Mr. Soto calls.

I let out an annoyed sigh. I've had enough upheaval in my life lately. I don't need anyone coming to Hogwash, trying to shake things up. Least of all me. I lost my one shot at love all too soon and now I have other, more important, things to focus on.

Leveling my gaze at the two women, I say, "It's too *hot* in this town for guys with flannel shirts."

"Firemen wear T-shirts too," Molly says as if she knows this firsthand.

Our volunteer crew consists of men old enough to be her grandfather, including Hank, Dick, and Buck, along with a few of the farm boys who're just barely eighteen.

"Firefighters sometimes have beards," Roxanne says as if that suits her best friend's fancy.

I snip, "But not of the attractive variety. Usually, those guys are also missing teeth."

"Sawyer has all his, mostly," Roxanne says.

"Grumpy Smurf," Molly mumbles in response to my comment.

I'm the only female member of the grouchy old codger club. The prospect of a newcomer waltzing into town, thinking he's the cock of the walk, rubs me the wrong way. Likely, he'll have tongues wagging and women distracted, which can only cause problems. I have enough of those.

Worry pinches my mind. It's probably too late to save the restaurant. I'm hanging on by a shoestring French fry, fending off foreclosure and floods during storm season. My house risks being blown away in a strong wind off the Gulf, which I can't risk now that I have a baby to take care of.

Rocking back on my heels, my mother was elbow and ankle deep in schemes while pushing me around in a baby buggy, but her sordid past started long before I came along. If that weren't the case, I'd understand why, in desperation, someone might resort to a life of crime.

Roxanne snaps her gum, jolting me. She asks, "Do you think he's a Tickle descendent?"

"If so, you'd think he would've made his claim by now, but sources say he's signing the paperwork on Monday," Molly says.

Roxanne edges toward the door.

"Mug," I call, gesturing she return it.

She hastily sets it on the counter by the cash register. It's still full, which is no surprise. Sweet tea is the safer, less rugged option here at the Grille.

The two women exit, heads bent together, as they speak in hushed tones, likely about the supposed handsome firefighter who possibly inherited the Tickle Chateau.

I'll believe it when I see it.

Heaps of paperwork remind me of adopting Leonie, who is hopefully napping peacefully. My hopscotch childcare situation is a temporary solution and I'll have to figure out something better, especially because I'd rather be with her than refilling sugar shakers.

It's the only thing that makes coffee at the Laughing Gator Grille palatable. Not that I sell much of it or much of anything. With a sigh, that needs to change too, otherwise, I might have to start writing my mother in prison and asking for tips—and I don't mean the kind I'd like customers to leave on the table.

# Chapter 2

## *Pancakes, Flapjacks, Hotcakes*

There is no end to the list of things I'd rather be doing right now. It spans from dreaming about being on the sailboat I someday hope to own, eating ribs and watching a game, to sitting in the doctor's office in a paper gown waiting for ... an exam that only men get when they reach a certain age for cancer detection and prevention.

Unfortunately, I fall into the category of needing a prostate exam early. I'm in my mid-thirties and am seriously avoiding it. I lost my father to the disease and because of this, I qualify for early screening, along with the dire warning that I may never have children. Not that I want them. Kids are needy, whiny, and sticky. At least the ones I've been around.

All the same, my mother claims that I'm a miracle baby.

The only miracle I'd like to experience is an end to the nightmare that was my marriage and divorce. So there won't be any children in the foreseeable future because first, I'd have to get married *again* and that's never happening *again*.

The only "I do" I'll be saying is, *I do want coffee. I do want paid vacation time. I do want a sailboat.*

Yet here I am, being not-welcomed by the faded, splintered, and partially busted Hogwash Holler sign. Instead of saying Hogwash with an O, part of the top is missing, so it looks more like a U. *Hugwash Holler.*

Being hugged by a swampy backwater town on the bayou isn't my idea of fun, but I've masterminded a payback plan to make this acquisition tolerable, potentially lucrative, and dare I say … diabolical. I am not above revenge after what Emberly did to me.

Instead of tapping the brakes and flipping a U-turn, I'll admit that curiosity spurs me forward along Metairie Road.

It's not every day you inherit an entire town.

There's a gas station, post office, library, car wash, and a town hall—all the usual small-town suspects. I spot a hair salon that may double as a craft store, given all the festive fall décor.

*Yeehaw…or not.*

A massive rotating mug of root beer greets me from the roof of The Penny Gamble, a soda fountain. That's old-fashioned but cool. Down the road is a Coffee Loft which looks new. However, everything in between is in a sad state of disrepair, including Cory's Automotive, which ironically boasts car repairs.

I hit a bump and my bag slides into the passenger side door of the rental truck—the thing is huge with knobby tires. Practically a monster truck. The only thing missing is neon paint and the word *Beast* on the side.

The Department of Public Works should repave the road or I should've rented a vehicle with better shocks, but it was all they had with four-wheel drive—a precaution in swamp country.

Considering I own the town, I wonder if I am the DPW.

*Woot … womp!*

As if trying to *under*do itself, Hogwash also boasts Cherry's

Vintage and Resale with an advertisement for black and white televisions. I've either stepped back in time or this place was forgotten by time.

Speaking of, the clock tower is a few hours off. I check the clock on the dash. Nine hours, to be exact. The Flying Pig Theater all but grovels for saving with plywood over the windows spraypainted with the words *Save the Pig!*

Main Street dead ends at Sunnyside Mobile Home Park & Camp Ground. You can take a right toward what looks like a farm road or a left. Hidden in the bramble is a small wooden sign that says *Shady Lane.* I peer down that way before taking the turn. It's covered by a tapestry of overgrown live oak trees dripping with Spanish moss. Bald cypress stands ankle-deep in water farther into the swamp before it fades into deep darkness and occupied by the kinds of giant lizards we don't have out west.

*Let's* not go!

I'm concerned that the community center doubles as a laboratory for creating experimental or illicit substances, given the state of the pool.

Pulling to the side of the road, as I see it, I have two choices: hit the accelerator and pretend that I was never here or carry out my evil scheme.

Plan A will probably keep me out of jail, but I'll always wonder—not about jail, but about Hogwash Holler and how I could've made my ex as embarrassed and subsequently miserable as she made me.

Plan B will probably result in me also banking some regrets, but what those are, I'm not sure. Avoiding tetanus or dysentery?

I'm not so much thinking it through as I am looking for a coin to toss. Plan A, heads. Plan B tails.

My chest lifts and expands as I draw a deep breath, the

kind I haven't been able to take in months. Not since I found out Emberly was drawing money out of my bank account and gambling with some guy in Reno on the weekends.

Then my phone rings, jarring me from thinking about why my inhales have been on the shallow side lately—not ideal in my line of work. Never mind a doctor's office to check on my prostate, I know well enough to chalk this up to stress.

I've been running on fumes lately.

My phone rings a third time. I'll admit that I'm surprised they have cell service out this way.

"Maddo," I answer—a habit I picked up from my father, who always answered by saying his name.

"Witt, where are you? I've been calling all morning." It's Captain Leyton from the Carson City FD who refers to me by my last name.

"You don't want to know," I mutter.

"As long as it's not in trouble."

I glance around at my surroundings. "That remains to be seen."

He proceeds to try to woo me into a temporary teaching position for a new crew posting that bridges a need in the wildlands between Reno and Carson.

Before I left, I told him I'd think about it, which I've postponed until now. An incoming text helps me put off my decision a little longer. The message says that the meeting with the lawyers was moved up to this morning. I thought I had until after lunch to officially claim the rights to Hogwash Holler—or get back on a plane and forget this ever happened.

Keeping one ear on what Leyton is saying and one eye on the map app on my phone, returns me to civilization. Just over half an hour later, I'm parked in front of Chandler & Associates Law Offices in New Orleans. This truck moves.

"When can I expect you back?" Leyton asks.

I stall, wishing I had a quarter on me. I'm based in Reno and his offer is more than decent, but like everything, there are pros and cons. On the upside, being asked to instruct means I'm qualified to teach a crew and respected enough for leadership—maybe become a captain myself one day. Plus, I'd make more money. The con is I can't do things my way—I tend to operate on instinct and think about the details later. In this role, it's *do things by the book* or have it thrown at me.

Leg jittering, I blurt, "I might take a little longer than expected. It looks like I have a bit of a project ahead of me."

Before I left, some might have called me a workaholic. I prefer to think of it as dedicated. Pouring myself into my job was better than the mess I was dealing with Emberly. For more than a minute, an hour, or a day, I want things to be stable. No drama. No chaos. No ex-wife.

"Remember when I was at the academy, like the fire safety rule to *Stop Drop Roll?* you taught us to *Stop Assess Act?* I stopped and now I'm assessing."

He pauses. "Smart not to rush into things."

"Especially this. It appears as if I inherited a town," I say slowly, deliberately, hardly believing it myself.

Or, more accurately, this was supposed to be Emberly's inheritance. It's more like a settlement because she didn't have the resources to pay back all she took from me, so she offered up Hogwash Holler. Must be a real prize if Princess Emberly didn't want it. My thoughts seep with sarcasm.

"A town?" he repeats.

"Correct."

"Is that possible?"

"Apparently."

"I take that to mean you need a bit of time to get your affairs in order," Captain Leyton says.

And have revenge on the woman who had an affair and nearly robbed me blind, but I digress.

We say our goodbyes and my phone beeps with another text. It's the lawyer asking for my ETA.

To be fair, Hogwash Holler wasn't a one-horse town—though it only has one stop light. In all honesty, I like small towns. Prefer them to the city even though I live in one.

The pace is slower, life is quieter and generally more peaceful.

Most real estate transactions can take place virtually with digital documents, but I quickly gather things in Cameron Parish are old school. Plus, transferring the heritor holding isn't an ordinary process.

About an hour later, the ink is dry on the certificate of rights to Hogwash Holler and I am now the conflicted owner of a small town.

Had I not been distracted by Leyton's call, maybe I'd already be heading back to Nevada. Had I been able to find a coin to toss, perhaps I'd be able to forget about what Emberly did.

But I can't and now that I own Hogwash Holler, her fate is sealed.

Returning the way I came, I don't stop until the town leers at me in all its faded glory.

"I apologize in advance that you'll be collateral damage, but it must be done," I mutter.

Yeah, I'm talking to the town.

A wooden alligator head that forms part of the sign for the Laughing Gator Grille seems to do just that. Laugh at me with its chipped teeth and sun-bleached paint.

"I'll be the last one laughing," I add, kind of sounding like a movie villain.

Maybe my blood sugar is low. All I've had today is coffee.

This place looks good and greasy. I take a wide turn into a parking spot in front of the diner's plate-glass windows.

Seemingly out of nowhere, a red Porsche approaches from the other direction and makes a sharp turn, nosing into the slot.

Slamming on the brakes, I lift my arms. "What gives?"

The ladder truck engineer in Carson City would envy the available on-street parking here. He wouldn't even have to bother himself with cars occupying tow-away zones. If this place even has a fire department—which should be at the top of my list of things to look into.

Well, except for this fiery little number. The rental truck is considerably larger than the Porsche Spyder, but the woman with wildflower blonde hair behind the wheel is persistent.

Like we're in a standoff in a dusty western town, neither one of us backs up.

She glares at me.

I flash a smug smile.

Our front bumpers are almost kissing.

She signals for me to move.

I wink.

I'm not one to pull an ace card, but I do own this town. Technically, the spot is mine.

The door to the Porsche flies open, missing the truck's front panel by a millimeter. The driver looks up at me with fire in her eyes. I brace myself for impact.

Instead, she leaves the car door hanging open, casts a glare over her shoulder in my direction, and marches into the restaurant.

Leaning back in the seat, I'm stunned at her audacity. Her beauty. But I can't let myself get distracted. That was aggressively bold.

Maneuvering the truck into a parking space that's safely

away from the Porsche, I do the courtesy of closing the vehicle's driver's side door so the battery doesn't die.

Taking my chances, I enter the Laughing Gator Grille.

The sizzle of bacon comes from beyond the order window behind the long counter. A song about the power of love recorded from before I was born and featured in one of my favorite movies of all time plays on the stereo.

No one fills the tables along the windows. A hefty man sits at the end of the counter, nursing a milkshake. A spindly woman sits on a spinning stool and snaps her gum. A plump woman stands behind the counter. Crudely written with pieces of tape across her apron is the name *Molly*.

She leans toward the thin woman and says, "I think that's him."

"The hot firefighter?" she asks.

Apparently, newcomers get noticed around here, whereas I'd expect the showdown between the massive truck and the little Porsche would've been the talk of the town—unless the driver is Hogwash Holler's resident untouchable rich girl princess. Suffice it to say I am not a fan. Emberly can take her frilly coffee drinks, her manis, pedis, and shopping addiction on a hike in the swamp.

If the Porsche Princess thinks she's in charge around here, she has another thing coming.

And here she comes, clocking in at least five foot ten with blonde hair and long legs, wearing a pageant winner smile and red lipstick. Her brown eyes land on me, and her expression falls.

Instead of taking a seat or storming outside to her vehicle, she, too, wears an apron. Only, instead of the cheapo tape job, hers is embroidered with gold thread and says *Honey*.

"What can I get you?" she asks as if prepared to reply by telling me to get lost.

Molly whispers, "I'll add him to my cart. One-click shopping."

I'm not the only one who heard. Honey has no shortage of sharp looks in her arsenal and fires one at Molly. She mouths, *No way.*

"I'll take a coffee and a menu." Then, as an afterthought, I add, "Please," along with a smile—sometimes you can't fight fire with fire.

She drops the ceramic mug on the counter with a thud and the coffee sloshes as she pours it.

"As they say, 'You catch more flies with honey.'"

With a strong Cajun accent, she asks, "Cream, milk, sugar?"

"No thanks. I drink it black."

All three sets of eyes are on me. Scratch that. Four. Even the guy at the end of the counter stares.

I shrug. "I like it bitter."

Honey lets out a laugh that isn't at all sweet. It's the sound of a woman who's been scorned ... or jaded.

As if anticipating that I won't be able to stomach the stuff, Molly says, "There's a Coffee Loft across the street."

Assuming Honey is the head honcho around here, I turn to her. "Sounds like your waitress is suggesting I visit your competition."

"We're all one big happy family here in Hogwash—" The end of her sentence dangles with the unspoken suggestion that outsiders aren't particularly welcome.

Conveniently, the documents in my truck make me the opposite of an outsider. I'm the owner.

"They have amazing jumbo beignet buns," Molly adds.

Honey not so subtly or delicately stomps on Molly's foot.

The thin woman at the counter says, "Have you tried the pumpkin-flavor?"

"They keep selling out, but I got one with the coffee-flavored glaze." Molly all but drools.

As if annoyed by the conversation about the coffee shop, Honey scrubs the counter next to the coffee maker as if it did something to offend her.

Molly clears her throat. "Since you're new here, everyone orders the pancakes. Honey is the pancake queen. They're her specialty."

Her scrubbing pauses as if she considers allowing the compliment to penetrate her armor.

"Let me guess, the secret ingredient is honey," I say, meeting her big brown eyes. I glimpse something in them—an old wound? Secrets? I can't quite put my finger on it, but they're not bitter like the coffee, which I'm enjoying despite the suggestion I add cream and sugar.

Everything about her is sweet except the scowl on her lips—her full red lips—and the way she drives that fast red car.

My gaze flits to a large gold trophy emblazoned with a racecar on the shelf behind her. The engraving reads *Honey Hamilton* and the year—about a decade ago.

Her gaze follows mine and her expression hardens. "What do you want?"

"Do you mean in general or from the kitchen? Actually, I want to know why you were about to knuckle up over the parking spot."

"We know all about guys who drive vehicles like that." She points out the window.

Molly whips her head around. "We do?"

"Vehicles like what?" I ask, eager to hear what she has to say because I know next to nothing about women who drive red Porsche Spyders, not that I'd admit that fact.

"Monster trucks."

"Hardly. It's a Ford F-450."

22

"It's lifted."

"It has four-wheel drive."

She snorts. "Obviously."

"It's a rental."

"Oh." That detail simmers her down.

I explain that I wasn't sure what kind of terrain to expect in Hogwash Holler, but leave out that I didn't imagine a gem like this would exist in such a small town. It's like meeting myself in a mirror, only she's far prettier. Not that I'm bad looking.

Honey is witty, gritty, and confident. Capable too. She can be a brat, but she also knows her manners and chooses whether to use them. She doesn't hold back the sass, but her name is Honey, so there's sweetness, thoughtfulness, and kindness inside. She knows her strengths and hides her weaknesses. She'd never ask for help but usually doesn't need it.

We're basically the same person. Not sure how I feel about that.

I point to the hardware behind her head. "Tell me about that trophy."

Leveling me with her gaze, she says, "The problem with monster truck drivers is they think they can just plow over anything in their way."

"Can't they?"

"Not if they still want a windshield." Ah, so she's vengeful too. My kind of woman. The guys back at the station all agree that my attraction to wild women will be my downfall.

"Technically, you don't need one."

Her smile is thin. "Slashed tires."

"Have you seen how thick they are?" I hold out my hands to demonstrate, not quite sure why I'm defending monster truck drivers. I have a fully outfitted Tacoma out west that's suited for off-roading because it helps with my job and recreational activities.

"Brake lines," she says, the words dropping like a threat.

Undaunted by our little game, I angle the menu in her direction. "I'll take the flapjacks."

"Pancakes," she says.

"Yeah, the flapjacks."

She shakes her head. "Want me to spell it for you? P-A-N-C-A-K-E-S."

Molly's head bobs between us as if she's soaking in this bit of banter.

"Hotcakes," I say, waggling my eyebrows at Honey to see how far I can push her. Yeah, I can play that game too.

"They're called pancakes," Honey says.

"Not where I'm from."

"And where's that?" Molly asks.

But I don't answer. Instead, I'm in a deadlock with Honey. Our eyes hold, neither of us looking away like we're in a staring contest, waiting to see the other one flinch, swerve, look away.

But she doesn't waver.

My gaze magnetizes to her, but those big brown eyes on mine mess with my pulse ... and I lose.

# Chapter 3

## *Two Cowpeas in a Pod*

**W**ith a huff, I stride into the kitchen. Antoine has the day off today, meaning I'm a full-time cobbler —not a shoemaker or baker of the popular dessert. But if I were ever to change the menu here, I'd add some kind of fruit cobbler served warm a la mode. My mouth practically waters. Most days, I don't get a break for lunch. But I mean that I'm cobbling together my entire life, including playing cook today.

The experts are wrong. There's no such thing as work-life balance.

This reminds me, I owe Molly *cream brool,* as she insists on calling it.

While the pancakes sizzle on the grill—they're not flapjacks —I scowl at the newcomer through the food delivery window.

Him, Hotcakes? *Non, non, non.* My buns-n-biscuits.

That reminds me, I need to make a new batch for tomorrow. But right now, I crack some eggs for the crème brûlée. I'm not a professional chef, novice home cook, or trained to make fancy desserts. However, I have a knack—some might say a taste—for preparing foods that are a degree better than edible.

But that's the only degree I have.

Barely escaping high school, the one thing I'm truly good at was a dream I had to let go of because of other people's poor decisions. Mr. Monster Truck out there with his firm muscles pressing against the hem of his T-shirt, and his arrogant smolder only drives home that point.

I wanted the parking spot closest to the Laughing Gator because I was late after racing back to Lexi and JQ's new house after forgetting to leave them with Leonie's diaper bag.

From the dining room, a cell phone rings, and then a deep voice says, "Maddo."

Not able to ignore the conversation and using context clues, it shouldn't surprise me that this guy answers his phone by saying his name. Who does that except for the cockiest of guys in movies? Maddo, the monster truck driver, that's who.

Technically, the Ford isn't a monster truck, but he was driving like he was at a rally. Must've been really hankering for caffeine and breakfast.

I want to let these pancakes cook until they turn into hubcaps and then toss them at Maddo's head like a series of frisbees, but I take a deep breath, roll my shoulders back, and lift my chin. I've dealt with worse, especially back in my racing days and more recently during the annual Hogwash Hunt.

Once a year, people descend on our town, thinking they have front-row rights, and then leave it in ruins. But I remind myself that their presence provides a little financial boost so I can scrape through the other eleven months.

I peer through the food delivery window. Molly and Roxanne speak in a hush, likely gossiping about our newcomer.

Maddo has a full head of brown hair, a fashionable amount of stubble, and blue eyes that are dark in the center with a lighter blue ring around the iris, reminding me of the circle on a peacock's feather. He smirks as if he caught me staring.

As if I'd waste my time.

Sizing him up is more like. If he wants to go head-to-head, all I need to do is give the Porsche an oil change and I'll leave him in the dust.

I've tried to get rid of the Spyder. No one will buy it from me—not that there's much of a market for sports cars in Hogwash. But even going farther afield, I've been refused at dealerships and private sales across the state. I'm marked with an X because a lot of big money was bet on me to go to nationals. I ended up having to use my regional winnings and entry fees to bail my mother out, which resulted in me being swamped with the Laughing Gator Grille, meaning they lost big. As if that weren't bad enough of a punishment, I'm forced to drive the thing. If you have a lead foot like mine, it's all too tempting to kick it past forty miles per hour, but I can't afford a speeding ticket.

Molly's head of red hair fills the food delivery window, interfering with my view. "That was some meet cute."

"More like meet rude," I mutter.

"But he's cute."

"Rude," I repeat as if we're arguing over crème brûlée pronunciation again.

The Laughing Gator Grille isn't a large establishment and by the way that the corners of Maddo's lips twitch from behind his coffee mug, he hears every word of our exchange.

After a beat, he calls, "I didn't see a sign that said *Porsche Parking Only*."

"Hmm. Could be that you need glasses."

He waggles his eyebrows at me. "Or it could be that I like what I see."

I roll my eyes. I've been in this business long enough not to trust a flirt.

"There was no rush for you to get back. I was holding down the fort," Molly says proudly, suggestively, as if Maddo and I were merely playing Monopoly with the parking spaces on Main.

I know his type. He thinks he's a gift to women across the world—cities and small towns, rich and poor alike. A real charmer with that arrogant smolder that gives him a license to flirt.

The smell of scorching cream reaches my nose. I dash back to the pot on the stove where I'd started the crème brûlée and scrap it, then begin again.

Thankfully, the little bubbles in the pancakes were slow to form because the grill wasn't yet at full temperature, buying me time. Take two: they're cooked to perfection as usual.

Pride keeps me from serving my sole customer—aside from Mr. Soto—cold pancakes. I all but bring them out with bells—that would include a dusting of powdered sugar, a perfect pat of butter, and a side of fresh mulberries. "Here are your *pancakes.* Can I get you anything else?"

He nods at the syrup and butter. "That'll be all. Thanks for the *flapjacks.*"

I narrow my eyes, convinced he only said that to irritate me. I don't make it a habit of sassing customers, but he dug his way under my skin, making me itchy all over. However, instead of coming back with a zinger, I won't waste my time and return to the kitchen to finish the crème brûlée.

Unfortunately, I don't have a blow torch, though one would come in handy today for more than caramelizing the sugar. I carefully brown the top of the custard under the broiler.

With a smile, I return to the dining room where Molly not-so-subtly watches the out-of-towner eat the pancakes as if she'll glean his life story by the way he cuts little triangles into the stack and lets the syrup drip off before he stuffs the bite into his mouth.

Actually, perhaps you can tell a lot about a person by how they eat. Namely, that he's full of himself.

I set the crème brûlée on the counter in front of Molly who sits only one spot away from Maddo.

She bounces to her feet and gasps. "You made me cream brool!"

"Crème brûlée," he and I say at the same time.

Our gazes meet and we exchange a glance akin to the one when we were both vying for the parking spot. But his blue eyes on mine send a flutter through me that makes me rethink the one thing I know about myself.

Honey Hamilton Fact Number One: I'm unflappable.

Right now, with that gaze on me, I feel very flapped. So flapped. Super flapped.

A female voice with a Louisiana accent that's the same as mine but older, says, "Honey, where's the fire?"

Maddo jumps to his feet, alert. "Is there a fire?"

Betsy, one of the hair stylists from across the street, and the sweetest of the busy bodies in town, looks Maddo up and down. "Ten alarm."

"That's not a thing," he says, wiping his mouth with a thin napkin.

Betsy's eyes get all swirly. "You're a ten out of ten."

He tilts his head. "I don't get your meaning."

I'd like to know what criteria Betsy uses to grade guys because I give him two stars at most. Maybe three because he has nice teeth. Looks like he flosses.

Maddo peers around as if not accustomed to how things work in the small town "Arrivals Terminal."

"I'm Maddock Witt, ma'am—friends call me Maddo. Nice

to meet you?" The greeting is a barely veiled question, as if he's not entirely sure what he's dealing with.

They shake hands, then Molly extends hers as if for a kiss on the top like in old black and white movies. I half expect her to fall into reverie and say, *Enchanté*.

To her credit, Betsy acts normal, well, normal for a woman in her late fifties with strikingly brassy hair, an intense enthusiasm for garden gnomes and gonks, and who knows more about everyone in town than they do themselves—I think she's been preparing to pass her crown to Molly.

Turning to me, Betsy says, "*Cher*, Jesse is on his way back from Marais Way. I suggest you address the way you parked your car."

I glance out the window. At least the door is closed. I'll admit I was in a snit when I left it cockeyed in the parking spot with the driver's side door ajar.

Molly, having practically licked clean the ceramic ramekin that held her crème brûlée, bounces to her feet and joins me behind the counter. "I got this."

Betsy is right. I'd better move my car before I lose points with Jesse. It's bad enough that I've been driving as much as I have lately. Unless it's raining, I walk everywhere because sliding behind the wheel makes me long for what I can't have. For the dream I gave up. It also puts me at risk for fines I can't pay.

I reluctantly go outside. The sixty seconds it takes me to properly park resets my bearings. My cheeks return to their natural shade, my breath comes easier, and my irritation notches down. Could be the itty bitty sock on the passenger seat. Somehow, Leonie always manages to lose one.

When I return, Molly and Betsy all but have Maddock cornered for an interrogation. Good.

"So you're a firefighter?" Molly twirls a curl of her red hair.

He bobs his eyebrows. "You've got that right."

Never mind fires, this guy is so full of himself, he's going to flood the town.

"Hotshot firefighter," I say under my breath while wiping the counter.

He turns to me, capturing my eyes. "Let's talk about how I'm hot."

My stomach tightens. "Let's not."

"You don't think I'm hot?"

"A cocky, arrogant city slicker is more like," I mutter, not wanting them to join Team Maddo.

"East side of the Sierra Nevadas—Carson Spur specifically —mountain country."

Betsy smiles. "I hear everything is bigger out west, fires included."

He winks. "It's not the size of the blaze, it's the power behind the one putting it out."

Both women's cheeks flush. I flip on the overhead fan, then take a sip of ice water. Must've turned up the grill too high.

Molly says, "I figured you were here for the hunt."

He nods. "I do hunt. Ducks and waterfowl mainly."

"I mean the scavenger hunt."

"It's a bit early for that," I say, since it's barely fall and the scavengers descend in January.

He tilts his head to the side in question, but his gaze travels to me, blanketing me with the kind of hazy heat that radiates from a bonfire even at a distance.

I busy myself with refilling the napkin dispenser even though only three have been used today.

Betsy shakes her head. "According to my sources, who we have here is Mayor Maddo."

Concerned that she may be experiencing confusion from prolonged exposure to hair-styling product fumes, I ask, "Betsy, can I get you anything to drink? Maybe some sweet tea, coffee, or—?"

Lexi strides toward us. Where did she come from? I didn't even hear the door open. I scold myself for being distracted.

My stomach plunges with worry about Leonie as I finish my sentence. "Root beer."

Lexi waves her hands as if telling me that there's a venomous snake by my feet. "Honey, I know that look. Not to worry. The lion cub is peacefully slumbering in Uncle JQ's arms while he rocks her gently. It's a sight to behold." She sighs in a way that only a woman in love can at the thought of her man cradling an infant.

Relief washes through me that Leonie is okay, but why is she here?

Lexi says, "Everyone knows the Penny Gamble has the best root beer. No offense."

"What are *you* doing here?" I ask Lexi, interjecting and giving her a tight-lipped look for trying to poach my customer.

She shrugs. "I had a pancake craving."

Turning to Maddock, I say, "See? Pancakes."

Lexi peers through the food delivery window. "Where's Antoine?"

"I gave him a day off. It was Laramie and Maybelle's birthday this past weekend and he needed to recover."

Lexi rubs her stomach. "I cannot imagine having twins."

Maddock says, "I can attest, the flapjacks were good."

As I clear his plate, my hand brushes his, sending a flush of agitation across my skin and straight up to my cheeks. I grab his fork away, resentful that he liked my pancakes. His lips puff with a smolder as if he noticed the effect he had on me.

My eyes dart everywhere but there. Well, except for now. And now. And—you get the idea.

"Flapjacks. Is that what we're calling them now?" Lexi asks.

"No. The menu is the same as it's always been," I say forcefully.

Molly chirps, "The cream brool is amazing."

Lexi squints as if trying to decipher the town gossip's words.

Eager to get Maddock out of here because of all the flapping happening inside, I take his nearly empty coffee mug, too.

"I thought you offered free refills." He points to the sign on the wall.

This time, I can't hold back. "Not to a cocky monster truck driver who thinks he can come in here and do whatever he wants, including calling my pancakes flapjacks."

"Who made you the language police?"

My hand flies to my hip. "My restaurant. My rules."

He lengthens his spine and juts his chin. "Whatever happened to the customer always being right?"

I point to another sign on the wall that the Coffee Klatch guys got me last Christmas. It says *The customer is always right except when they're wrong.*

Everyone stares at us as if watching a tennis match. This could be the winning stroke for Hogwash or the losing one for customers, depending on which side they're rooting for.

Eyes fixed on me, practically giving me a sunburn, Maddock says, "Wait. Don't answer that. My town. My rules."

A low, "Oooh," choruses in the dining room. Then, everyone falls silent.

All I can hear is my heartbeat in my ears and see the blaze in his eyes.

Where's my carefully cultivated cool? I'm flapping and flustered right now, which makes me feel like that tennis ball is bouncing around inside me.

"I was here first." I flip my hair and walk the short distance to the coffee maker, then dump it down the drain while staring him down. "No. Service. For. You."

"She does make the best pancakes. You'll be missing out," Betsy says.

Lexi squints. "He's the new mayor, huh? Not by my vote. I elected Chick Jagger."

I want to thank them both for siding with me.

"My rogue rooster?" Molly asks. "If I find out who put him on the ballot—"

Roxanne coughs into her hand.

We all stare at her for a long moment in disbelief.

I say, "If animals are allowed to be mayor, my cat Minou would make a great candidate."

Maddock looks up at the ceiling. "Where am I?"

"Hogwash Holler," we all say at the same time.

He nods slowly. "The name really says it all."

"And you recently came into some property within the township," Lexi says slowly as if peeling back layers of the truth.

He nods equally slowly. "That's right."

"And that includes the chateau?" Molly asks.

He rubs the back of his neck. "It would seem so. The lawyer reviewed it all with me, but I haven't quite taken everything into account."

"If you're Tickle's heir, of course, it would include his former residence."

No wonder he's pompous. People in Hogwash loved Hogan, but it was in retrospect—according to accounts, the man was cantankerous, a sore loser, and prone to wandering around town at night, scaring the ghosts after imbibing enough *Fifolet* to drown a gator.

"Congratulations," I say dryly because although the name

*chateau* implies a posh location, he'll be mighty disappointed when he sees the state of the once grand property.

Lexi says, "Honey, why don't you show our newcomer over there?"

I choke on ... nothing. Air goes down the wrong pipe. When I catch my breath, I ask, "Me? Is this revenge for insisting JQ show you around town?"

Her grin is impish. "How would that even work?"

I'd pledge to get her back for getting me back if she didn't help look after Leonie.

If this is true, Maddock has the key to a door that ought to remain closed. There's no treasure. But there are treasure hunters. And secrets, lies, loss. Tears even. But no treasure. At least not anymore. I would know.

People come and go, either dismissing us locals or using us with the hopes of getting treasure insight, but I've got nothing other than this secondhand life, so he won't be getting anything from me.

Maddock tosses two twenties on the counter, which is more than double his tab. We all stare at it, more accustomed to smaller bills, coins, and pocket lint.

"Yeah. Let's go check it out." His gaze lands on me expectantly.

Maddock is annoyingly handsome and he knows it, which grinds my gears. I'm a warm cucumber. Nothing cool about me right now.

"Betsy, didn't you need help with something?" I hedge.

She waves her hand dismissively. "That was just Hogwash. I wanted to see this hotcake that rolled into town." She bats her eyelashes. "You have very thick hair. Come by the salon when you need a trim. Thelma would love to meet you."

I highly doubt that. Thelma is about as friendly as the crocogator.

"Go on. I'll mind the Grille if you make me another cream brool," Molly says.

Why isn't anyone helping me out here?

"Come on. Show me around," he says with the smug kind of smile of a guy who's used to a female feeding frenzy.

"You're going to regret this," I say, but the flutters inside make me wonder if I'm talking to myself or him.

"Y'all are like two cowpeas in a pod. Now off you go," Betsy says.

For being such a small woman, she has a surprising amount of strength when she shoves us together.

I stumble in my wedge heels.

Maddock grips my arm to steady me, making the flapping inside extend to my fingers and toes. Not at all liking the way that feels or what it could mean, I yank my arm away.

Molly and Lexi all but thrust me out the door.

"No using the grill until I get back," I holler.

But the three women already have their heads together, gossiping.

I can practically hear them now, speculating about which one of us will swing—or knowing their romantic notions of fire-fighter hotcakes—fall first. It won't be me. I've dated a few guys, they come and then they always go. This one will be no different.

# Chapter 4

## *A Revenge Plot WIP*

ike we were kicked out of the restaurant for bad behavior, Honey and I careen toward each other on the sidewalk. We stop short of making contact much like our vehicles earlier. But it's like there's an invisible elastic tension between us.

One hard snap and ... I wonder what would happen.

Then I remember why I'm here and it's not to woo a woman. More like making one regret the day she betrayed me.

No longer wearing her apron, Honey brushes off her denim skirt that gives way to a pair of long, tanned legs and wedge sandals with red painted toenails that match her car.

*Vavavoom.*

I smooth my hand down my shirt.

She glances at her feet, then her car, before her gaze darts across the street, and then back at the sidewalk. She's looking everywhere but at me.

Something sparks inside, making me want to change that, but then I remember the last time I let a woman lure me in.

A welcome fall breeze ruffles the palms and the waxy leaves on the myrtle trees, cooling me off from within.

Honey marches over to her car, opens the glove box, and pulls out a lollipop. I half expect her to offer me one, but she puts it in her mouth, drawing my attention there.

Unfortunately, the air is now still.

And I'm burning up again.

In an annoyed tone, she says, "Let's get this over with."

Something about the lollipop, her lips, and her no-nonsense attitude messes with my pulse.

She stops short and I nearly bump into her.

Not unexpectedly, I receive a scowl as if it's my fault she decided not to keep walking.

A magnet draws me close while an invisible force seems to push me away. The tension makes me imagine what her smooth skin would feel like under my calloused fingers, her silky hair in my hand, and her lips ...

*Whoa there, Hotcake.*

A woman with a cane, toting what looks like a battery-operated dog, crosses the street toward us.

Hardly moving her lips, Honey says, "Looks like you're getting the full Hogwash Holler greeting committee. Buckle up."

"Honey, is that your red car?" the older woman asks.

"Yes, Mrs. Halfpenny."

"Earlier, I saw a truck almost plow into it."

"That truck?" Honey points with her lollipop.

She squints. "I can't be sure. They all look the same to me."

I start to protest, but the animatronic dog barks.

Mrs. Halfpenny stiffly crouches down and soothes the toy. "Frodo, *there there*. It's okay. I won't let him run you over with that big mean truck." Straightening, she says, "Who are you?"

"My name is Maddock Witt, ma'am."

She peers up at me through thick glasses. "I'm Shirleen Halfpenny and I have my good eye on you. Don't miss a trick. Understand?"

Despite how very seriously I take her cautionary comment, given that she thinks all trucks look the same and thinks her battery-operated dog is real, I fight a smirk. "I understand, ma'am."

Mrs. Halfpenny looks at Honey for a long moment and then turns to me. "Hogwash Holler isn't the kind of place where matches are made. Rather, hearts are broken. Now that you've manned up, I don't want to have to break any legs. So if you try to run off again—" She brandishes her cane.

Small towns are known for having characters, but this place is something else.

In a much sweeter voice, Mrs. Halfpenny asks Honey, "Did you save any bacon for Mr. Frodo?"

"I'll bring it by later."

"Good. Someone has to bring home the bacon around here and help a girl out." Mrs. Halfpenny looks me up and down, then nods at Honey before stumping off.

"What was that all about?" I ask, walking toward the truck.

"She thinks you left me high and dry."

"Why would she think that?"

Honey's shrug is lethargic. Then the comment about broken hearts floats back to me. Maybe someone special in her life left, leaving her bitter. I know the feeling.

I open the passenger door to the truck.

Shaking her head with more vigor than the shrug, she stands there, sucking on her lollipop. "I'm not riding with you."

"I don't know where I'm going."

She points down the street. "Drive that way until you hit the bayou."

"And have to call a tow truck?"

"You said yourself that you rented this monster because it has four-wheel drive."

Touche. I'll check the brake lines just to be safe.

She shifts her weight. "The chateau isn't hard to find. You don't need a tour guide."

"But Molly said you're the best."

"Molly doesn't know everything—" Honey tilts her head as if reconsidering that.

"You still didn't tell me about the trophy."

"Ancient history."

The window of the Laughing Gator Grille fills with three women, all staring at us as if waiting for Honey to get in the truck.

"Or you could go face them." Plastering on a smile, I proffer a cheerful wave.

"Fair point." She gets into the truck.

I close the door, wondering which one of us will lose this proverbial game of chicken. Honey is in it to win it, but I'm no slouch either. She has a strong will. Is a bit wild. I remind myself why I'm here ... and who got me into this mess. A growl escapes at the thought of Emberly.

When I get in the driver's seat, her honeysuckle scent fills the cabin and I figure there has to be some sweetness hidden under her sassy exterior.

After I back out of the parking spot, I continue down Main Street. "Not much here, huh?"

She huffs as if affronted—like only residents are allowed to comment on the town's shortcomings. "There's plenty. Hogwash Holler has Hallmark Town potential but a home video budget. If you squint, you can imagine fresh paint, flowers instead of weeds, and adorable shops instead of the This & That."

"Hugwash Holler definitely has character."

"Hogwash," she says.

"The sign says Hugwash."

"It's Hogwash and we're Hoggers."

"Huggers." I veer left down Shady Lane, passing under the canopy of live oaks, dimming the interior of the truck. "I figured I'd get a hug while we're exploring my new place."

"Not on your life. Hoggers aren't the cuddly type unless you want to cozy up with a gator."

"Sounds like you're saying, *Huggers*."

"I have an accent, but—"

Which is adorable when she's not being so feisty, but it draws me like a flame. "I've noticed."

She turns her head in my direction as if I'm teasing. "I've lived here for a long time It's Hogwash."

"I like Hugwash better. I'll make a motion to officially change it."

"You're not actually the mayor."

No, but I own this place. I wonder if there are any rules about changing the town's name.

Honey crunches the remainder of the lollipop in her mouth. "This isn't like the whole pancakes versus flapjacks thing."

"We can agree to disagree. Or we could settle on Hotcakes." I wink.

She snorts an exhale through her nose as if beyond frustrated with me trying to irritate her. But as I see it, we're on equal footing. She has her feminine wiles and my only tool is to rile her up, making us even.

The tunnel of tree branches dripping with moss opens to a slight clearing, but the surrounding old live oaks climb toward the sky as if reaching through the canopy of branches and leaves for a skylight, leaving us in the gloom.

"Now where do I go?" I ask, wincing because she'll probably tell me to go back the way I came. Meaning, leave Hogwash.

"There's nothing out this way other than the Tickle Chateau, an old fort called the Metairie Stronghold, the graveyard, and the swamp."

I'm starting to wonder if I got a bad deal in the divorce settlement. This was supposed to be payment for all the stolen money and damages, but by the looks of things, this place has seen more than a few storms and lost a battle with the bayou.

"So you're a Tickle?" Honey asks with a combination of hesitancy and defiance in her voice.

"No. My last name is Witt."

"But you're the heir to the estate, so you must be related."

"It's a long story. But the one I want to hear is about this place."

"You inherited it, surely you know the history and about the hunt."

I don't, but I'll let her fill my silence how she wants.

"Thousands of people have visited Hogwash Holler, seeking fame and fortune. No one has found the treasure, no less the inheritance. But they all left town in worse shape than when they arrived. It's broken families, caused rivalries, bitterness, and bankruptcy. That wasn't Hogan Tickle's intention."

The truck's tires crunch over fallen branches and dead leaves before a large structure with ivy creeping along its columns and a broad front entryway covered in moss comes into view. Broken windows, sooty mildew, and tarnished ironwork make me think the place is the set for a horror movie. If we're the characters, the viewers are telling us to turn back.

"It's kind of spooky," I say.

Honey laughs. "Don't tell me you're scared."

"Pfft. I run into burning buildings for a living and before that, I battled wildfires. I can handle this."

"It's not haunted." She says with a smile as if to imply the opposite.

Except that some of the choices I've made in my life linger like ghosts, and I wonder if Honey has a few specters of the past who occasionally show themselves. I'm not rethinking my decision to take on this town but am reconsidering my tactics. Above all, I wish I'd never gotten involved with Emberly.

"You say it's not haunted like you're reverse trying to convince me not to go in."

"That's like calling a pancake a flapjack."

I grunt. "So you're not scared?"

"Nothing scares me, Maddock." The way she says my name suggests the opposite. Like she's trying to be brave. Not because she's afraid of me but of what would happen if she let down her guard.

"This will be an adventure." My gaze holds hers for one lingering moment before I get out of the truck.

Honey exits before I can open the door for her. Breezing past me, she strides toward the chateau. The falling sunlight makes the stained glass window on the north side of the house glow like a beacon.

Honey picks up a peacock feather and twists it in her hand. During wildfires out west, birds are always in need of new homes. After the last months of settling the divorce, I feel like I'm trying to outrun a fire and find someplace to land. The stone steps are slick with slimy moss, but even in the wedge sandals, Honey's steps are sure.

I say, "I take it you've been here before."

"Many times."

"Was it a high school dare to come here at night or something?"

"No, that was to sleep in the graveyard."

"Which you did?"

"Of course."

Honey gestures for me to open the big wooden door. I take out the key.

She says, "You won't need that."

"It's unlocked, meaning anyone can come in and rob the place."

Her smile suggests that I should know the answer. "Generally speaking, yes."

I shoot her a quizzical look but stick close to her as we enter a cavernous rotunda-style entryway with a chandelier overhead. It's barely hanging on as if someone once literally swung from it.

I say, "Looks like a fun party."

"Depends on your definition of fun."

Everything is damp. Wallpaper peels in long sheets from the plaster. Moldering leaves carpet the floor and the actual carpet squelches underfoot. Nature and a pack of wild boars hardly spared a single item, fixed or decorative. Why would Emberly let a place like this fall to ruin?

Honey juts her hip like she's bored and would rather be anywhere but here. Yet, in her gaze, I see sadness as if memories filter back, but instead of saving them in a scrapbook, it's like she'd rather toss them in a fire.

"What happened?"

Her expression falters. "To me?" she asks as if that's none of my business.

I'll bookmark that for later. "To this place."

She answers with a question as if running a background check. "What are you really doing here?"

"A revenge plot."

"I can't tell if you're serious."

"Oh, I assure you, I am." Emboldened by my purpose, I stride deeper into the house but then glance over my shoulder.

For a fraction of a second, Honey looks like a lost little girl who's not eager to take a step further.

I ask, "How about you? What are you doing here?"

"The better question is, why didn't I ever leave Hogwash?" she mutters.

The chateau consists of high ceilings, pillars, and furnishings with ornate details. It's part opulent and part gaudy and all French Renaissance style. I imagine antiques of the crystal and gilded gold variety once covered every available surface.

"Looks like a pack of raccoons has been occupying the place."

Honey replies, "Worse than raccoons. Just about everything that wasn't nailed down was pilfered."

I'm not sure what's worse than raccoons, but we pause in front of the fireplace with a carved wooden and marble mantle. The air is thick with humidity and there's no need for a fire, but something stokes inside. The same thing messing with my pulse.

Honey looks up at me with her big brown eyes. "My first draft failed and I never got back to writing the story."

Picking up on her analogy and recalling what Mrs. Halfpenny said about broken hearts, I reply, "I like to think of life as a work in progress."

She takes a few steps away. "Mostly just work."

"Is that how you deal with a broken heart?"

Honey gazes toward the window and snorts. "Don't believe everything Mrs. Halfpenny says or sees, if that robot dog is any indication."

"I do okay reading people on my own."

"If you mean that you think I have a broken heart, you're mistaken. I have a broken life. But a good one. I accept the cards that I was dealt—" Her gaze drifts to the large round table in the corner. "I don't want pity or help."

"I wasn't offering."

She sniffs as if not expecting me to say that and lengthens her spine.

Recalculating my approach because I'm punch drunk on the bayou breeze and Honey's scent, I say, "Maybe I want *your* help."

Her eyebrows shoot up. "With your revenge plot?"

"Possibly. We'll see how things unfold." I lift my shoulder.

Pain splits her expression and then just as quickly disappears. "If you're looking for me to do anything illegal—"

I pump my hands. "Whoa. Let's not get carried away."

Honey tilts her head as if waiting for me to explain.

The corner of my lip twitches. "To carry this off, I'll need a steady supply of flapjacks."

She lets out a frustrated exhale. "You're a twit, you know that?"

"Nah, I'm a Hugwash Hugger." I open my arms because despite the way people may perceive me—Leyton says I'm cocky—I recognize when someone needs a hug.

Her nostrils flare.

I wiggle my fingers, indicating she come in close, but she doesn't budge.

A light flashes through the window—police red, blue, and white.

Almost reflexively, Honey coils like she's about to make a run for it, but then relaxes, wearing a smile that hides secrets. She stares through the window as if defying the odds that we're going to be booked for trespassing.

"Are we in trouble?" I ask, joking.

"Everyone in Hogwash Holler is. It just depends on how much peace you can amass to cope with that fact."

My pulse lurches. I wonder about Mrs. Halfpenny's comment. I wouldn't need a cane to break legs if some guy ran off on Honey. She's defensive, but there's a reason for that. Whoever hurt her deserves worse than whatever they've gotten.

I rock back on my heels. But why am I considering defending her? Maybe she's right and I am in trouble.

# Chapter 5

## *Breaking & Entering*

An imposing figure fills the opening of the chateau's front door. During another chapter of my life, this would be a problem. I forcibly tell myself not to make a run for it on pure instinct.

Whereas I'm usually relaxed, in my hard won unflappable way, Maddock seems completely unphased by the flashing lights and the presence of the law officer blasting us with a flashlight.

I wince, shielding my eyes.

Jesse says, "Oh, Honey. It's you. Didn't see your car outside." His tone suggests he did see it on Main Street earlier.

"Sorry about that. Won't happen again. Drivers from out of town don't always heed our parking rules, so—"

"There was no *Porsche Only* parking sign." Maddock turns to Jesse and gives him a chin nod.

Jesse surveys him carefully and says, "That's something you'd have to take up with the mayor, Honey."

Hand on hip, I say, "Unfortunately, I haven't seen Mayor Jagger lately."

Jesse shifts uncomfortably. "What are you doing out here?"

"Just giving a tour." I gesture at our surroundings and at the man who came protectively to my side like we're accomplices in a crime. A pleasant plume of cedarwood and smoke wafts my way—the same scent permeating the truck. It makes me twitchy inside.

The spotlight turns to him. "Sir, I'm Maddock Witt."

"Jesse Lawson. Deputy Sheriff." The nod of recognition he gives Maddock makes me wonder if I'm missing something. He's the heir, but he said he's not related to Tickle. Perhaps he's a debt collector. My guilty conscience rises like a zombie out of a grave.

"Nancy at dispatch said a suspicious vehicle with out-of-state plates passed down this way. Just following up."

"It's a rental. Figured I'd get four-wheel drive because I wasn't sure what to expect. That was all they had available," Maddock supplies.

"Smart man." Jesse looks around. "I came down here often enough while investigating the Bling Ring, but I haven't been inside for years."

Me neither.

"My cousin Sawyer and I used to rile each other up, claim the place was haunted. We'd ignore the *No Trespassing* sign and sneak in." He points. "Looks like our spray paint still stains the plasterboard walls in the dining room."

The flashlight grazes the words *Break the Law*.

"Jesse hasn't always worn a uniform," I say.

"And you didn't always wear your seatbelt." He tips his head knowingly at me.

"Times change," I answer.

"Except on the town clock."

"Which was also your doing," I say.

We both chuckle.

Jesse adds, "It's a wonder we made it to the other side. Sawyer just barely. How about your cousin?"

"Last I heard she went north, scamming wealthy golfers by posing as an innocent drink cart girl and working her way into affluent social circles."

"Sounds just like the Queen of Hearts," Jesse says.

"Sounds like a high-maintenance princess like my ex. However, she was clingy, and not independent-minded enough to con golfers out of their gold. I vowed to be a casual connections-only type of guy from now on. Never again will I enter into a serious relationship," Maddock says as if trying to convince himself.

"It's a wonder she and Sawyer didn't end up together," I echo.

"Nah, he's got his sights set more locally."

Maddock says, "I take it you weren't exactly exemplary citizens."

Wishing I could shed that part of my history, I snap, "Past tense."

"These days Mrs. Halfpenny keeps us honest." Jesse points the flashlight's beam around the space, inspecting it. "If our mayor wasn't a rooster, I'd petition to raise funds to repair the clock among other things."

"How exactly does that fly?" Maddock asks.

"It's Hogwash," Jesse and I echo.

"Hugwash," he counters.

Not privy to our previous conversation, Jesse paces a short circle through the room and says, "I always had a feeling Honey would end up living over on Marais Way."

I let out a peel of delirious laughter. "Me over there?"

Jesse juts his chin westerly. "It's where the other pageant queens live."

"We both know I don't belong in the bougie part of town."

"Like you said, times change." Jesse hangs his thumbs in his belt loops.

At this point, I can't take any more change. I'd like time to slow down. For things to stay still and let me catch my breath. I turn toward the door. "I was just leaving."

Maddock mounts the stairs. "I'm not done checking out the house."

With big brother caution in his voice, Jesse says, "You can't walk back. There have been crocogator sightings."

"Shouldn't the mayor do something about that?"

Jesse winces. "I'm afraid Chick Jagger was its lunch."

"In that case, it looks like we need a new mayor. I nominate my cat," I mutter the last part because of the absurdity of the concept, no less Hogwash residents electing a chicken in the first place.

"Maddock, it was nice to meet you. Congratulations. If there's anything I can do to be of help, please don't hesitate to ask."

Jesse extends his hand to shake.

Maddock replies, "I appreciate your service, especially you checking up on things. That's always a good sign."

"That's what I'm here for. Do you plan to fix up the place?" Jesse gestures to the chateau.

"The original plan was to bulldoze it, but—"

I gasp. "You can't do that."

"Why?" he asks as if unable to fathom my objection.

Me neither, but the words slipped out. I shift uncomfortably, certainly not attached to the chateau. "I've considered taking a sledgehammer to it on more than one occasion, but it's part of history."

"It's rotting into the ground."

"Maybe if you do a little digging, you'll find the treasure," Jesse says.

"There's no treasure," I say, my tone flat.

"You don't know that for sure. I broke the Bling Ring and found Mrs. Swan's engagement ring," Jesse says, referring to a recent public scandal and a personal case.

Maddock asks, "If there were, wouldn't it go to me since I'm now the owner of Hogwash Holler?"

Never mind delirious laughter, I all but cackle. "You can't own a town."

The two men exchange a glance.

"Of course you can," Jesse says.

The corner of Maddock's mouth peels back with a grin. "Signed the paperwork today."

"So you're the mayor? I'd rather have the rooster in charge," I say, feeling prickly about this whole situation, mostly because of the way Maddock looks at me and my traitorous body's response.

"No, I'm the owner," he clarifies.

Jesse holds his hand up with a wave and exits as if he wants no part in our disagreement, leaving Maddock and me in near darkness without the glow of the flashlight.

The floor creaks under his weight when he takes a few steps toward the window.

"I inherited the town in the divorce settlement from my lying, cheating ex-wife."

"Hence the revenge plot."

"Exactly."

"But how would that work?"

"The original plan was to expose her, humiliate her, and then secretly burn it to the ground."

I narrow my gaze at him. "I thought you said you're a firefighter."

"I meant figuratively."

"Ruin the place and bring disgrace to her family name under the guise of being the good guy? That's diabolical."

"Trust me, she's worse."

Maddock may be an obnoxiously arrogant nitwit, but I don't like the idea of someone betraying him. I know the feeling and wouldn't wish it on anyone. "You sound bitter."

"Quite."

"The bitter heir. If you were to succeed in your plan, do you think that would make you feel better?"

"I never said I felt bad."

"You must, considering you hatched a plot to destroy a town, never mind the collateral damage. Real people live here, you know." I really don't like that part of his master plan.

He surveys our surroundings with disappointment. "Yeah, and it turns out someone already did the dirty work."

"This is Hogwash. Get used to it. But this means you'll need a new plan to sabotage your ex. I have a love-hate relationship with this town, but you're not ruining it."

He makes a sound as if that's not off the table but says, "I'll come up with something."

He's quiet for a long beat as if tapping into options for Plan B.

Instead of leaving as planned, lest I go the way of Chick Jagger, I gravitate deeper into the house, recalling the shadows in my life that follow me even on sunless days.

Faint footsteps follow me until they catch up. Maddock stops by my side where I look at the grandfather clock.

His gaze strays to me as if wondering if I'll give him the time of day.

Not a chance, buddy.

He says, "I can see how it was once grand."

"Times change," I repeat.

"I wonder if fixing it up and bringing this place back to life would be a more apt act of revenge."

"Restoration as an act of retaliation? That's a novel idea."

"Like I said, I'm a work in progress." He winks.

I tell my smile muscles to stand down, but they defy my orders.

A sliver of light shining through the stained glass window separates Maddock and me. I tell myself it's more than space and light and time. There are circumstances in my life that prevent me from even entertaining so much as a hug with this man.

The corner of his mouth lifts. "Jesse was right. You have a pageant winner smile."

I scoff. "Those days are long behind me."

"But you said it yourself. Times change."

"Exactly. I'm about as far from being a true pageant winner as the clock tower is to telling the correct time."

Maddock tips his head from side to side. "Except twice a day."

A sinister part of his potential plot slithers into my thoughts. "Do you want to use me to make your ex jealous?"

He chuckles. "Aren't you deviously minded?"

"It wouldn't be the first time," I mutter.

Maddock squints his eyes as if he's trying to get a better look at me. "No. I'd never do that. I wasn't sniffing around or inquiring. Seeing if you were interested. If I was, you'd know it. Plus, due to the aforementioned ex, if I were to become involved with someone, it would be a no-strings-attached arrangement."

My stomach doesn't sink. I'm just hungry. "Lucky for you, I come with a lot of strings."

"So, no casual dating for you."

"And nothing serious for you."

"We won't be taking part in anything romantic."

He winks. "Definitely not."

"There's a reason I'm single. You're not going to change that no matter what you do."

"I wouldn't dare. You're looking for someone honorable, long-term. I respect that." His head bobs like it's settled.

"That's right. You must really hate your ex if you were willing to ruin Hogwash," I say with an air of protection.

"I didn't say I hate the people in it."

"Give it time," I murmur because right now I'm not too pleased with Molly, Betsy, or Lexi for throwing me into this blaze.

He smirks. "But you like me."

I back up, nearly falling into a chair with the stuffing missing and the springs exposed. "I do not."

Maddock reaches for my hand, but I play keep-away.

He says, "You just don't realize it yet."

I huff, then echo what he said, "Definitely not."

His eyes hold on me for a long moment. "Finish showing me around."

No *please*? I'll *show* him. "Fine. We'll go to the graveyard."

"Cemetery," he counters.

"Grave. Yard," I practically growl.

He makes his voice airy like a ghost and says, "Cemetery."

Graveyards are graveyards and pancakes are pancakes, and I could do without the newcomer to town. Because this one almost sends me up in flames.

# Chapter 6

## *Kissing is Gross*

Being around Honey is like walking into a rosebush, though her scent is closer to honeysuckle. And this property is anything but sweet. Vines and creeping plants slink and hang from the cypress and tupelo trees.

The air is thick and stagnant. Slime pools along the edges of the murky swamp. This is the kind of place where people disappear—whether because they're eaten by an alligator or fall into a pit of quicksand, I'm not sure.

Dead leaves rustle from beyond a thick mat of greenery.

"Watch your step. We have cotton mouth snakes around here," Honey says.

"We have rattlers out west. At least they have the decency to warn us."

"Got those too," Honey warns.

A squawk comes from a nearby tumble of weeds and I startle slightly.

"It's just a peacock." Honey waves the feather she picked up earlier.

"I thought chickens were in charge around here."

"You mean Chick Jagger. It would be a shame if the crocogator got him."

"Do you mean crocodile?"

"Crocogator."

"Alligator?"

"It's a hybrid and albino," she says matter of fact.

I squint because that sounds an awful lot like a tall tale someone from a small town would tell an outsider. All the same, I keep a better eye on my surroundings—ahem, including Honey. Wouldn't want either one of us to get lost or separated.

"A hybrid alligator and crocodile that has white hide? Is that even possible?"

"Anything is possible in Hogwash." She seems unfazed by that fact, the humid air, and the squelchy ground beneath our feet even though she's wearing wedge sandals with little straps around her ankles that make me wonder about her being a pageant queen. Her legs are long, toned, and tan. She steps lightly and almost seems to glide rather than stomp like she did on the sidewalk earlier.

I'm not sure whether she's wary of outsiders or if her gaze darting to me and then quickly flitting away means something else. Something I should not be thinking about because Honey made it clear that this isn't Hugwash ... or Kisswash.

"Should we go back and get the truck?" I ask, concerned for her with the muck underfoot.

She says, "We wouldn't be able to go much farther than this, anyway."

We stop in front of a fallen stone portico surrounded by a wrought-iron fence that reminds me of a set of crooked teeth.

"I can't decide if we're on the site of ancient ruins from history books or a horror film set," I say.

Starting forward, she glances over her shoulder, and with a

challenge in her voice, she says, "Come on. Unless you're scared."

No sooner does she challenge me, than she skids in a slick of mud. Like the gallant fellow I am, I loop my arm around her and use my body to steady her. Face to face, we're a feather apart. I catch her gaze after she avoided mine for so long outside the restaurant. They shine in the dim light under the trees and clouds. My breath falters and my pulse turns irregular.

After a long beat, Honey presses her palm to my chest. She glances at it and then up at me.

My voice is rough when I say, "I'm not scared of anything. Not even of your lips on mine."

She jerks back. "Ew. Kiss you? No way. Gross."

"Why would kissing me be gross?"

"You're probably all slimy and—" She wiggles her fingers and wrinkles her nose.

"Yeah, well, kissing you would be like getting bitten by an alligator."

We sound like a pair of bickering children.

She continues into the cemetery, stepping more carefully now. "Have you ever been?"

"Kissed?" I hold back a large tuft of elephant grass, blocking the path, and gesture that she proceeds.

She grunts. "No. Have you ever been bitten by an alligator?" But before I answer, as if still thinking about the prospect of kissing, she says, "Just no. Gross. Worst idea ever."

A beat passes between us and she fights against having her eyes all over me—instead focusing on the dead air between us.

I say, "But you were thinking about it."

"Was not. You brought it up. That means you were thinking about it."

"How could I not? You know you want me."

"You are so full of yourself."

I duck under a thick blanket of creeping ivy. "I'm getting Indiana Jones vibes."

"Watch your step, Short Round."

"No, way, I'd be Indy. He's a dude. You'd be the love interest."

I expect her to turn around and shoot me a glare. Instead, she lets out a robust laugh that scatters a gathering of crows. Her response suggests that love isn't part of her story these days. Unless there are strings attached.

Instead, she says, "*Allons.*"

"Allen? I thought we were going to pay our respects to Hogan Tickle."

Honey's Cajun accent is thick and I find myself enjoying the rhythm and occasionally having to decipher her meaning like a puzzle ... or a riddle.

She repeats, "*Allons.* It's Cajun or Franglais. Whatever you want to call it. It means *Let's go.*"

Clouds obscure the sun as it dips toward the west. It's later in the day than I'd like when visiting a cemetery. The path is overgrown and the long grass tickles my ankles. Unlike the cemeteries at higher elevations, the above-ground burial sites here are marked with chipped and broken stones like the dead aren't really at rest. A massive live oak hangs over one section like it's given up. A gust of wind clears the swampy air, replacing it with a salty brine. In the distance a sheet of water gleams. Only now getting the lay of the land, I had no idea we were so close to the coast.

When we reach the back, Honey stops in front of a mausoleum with embellishments carved into the stone. The top comes to a peak and underneath reads the name, *Hogan Darius Tickle,* and the years: *1890-1963.*

"He was the finder of Hogwash Holler."

Not sure I heard correctly, I ask, "Do you mean founder?"

"This isn't a cream brool situation."

"Flapjacks," I say, catching the reference to different terms and pronunciations of words from earlier.

She scowls at me but even in the fading light of the day, I see a shimmer in her eyes. "Pancakes. But as I was saying ... Way back in the way back—"

I point to the gravestone. "Sometime in the early 1900s?"

She nods. "Hogan Tickle's adventures led him in search of pirate treasure. Some say he was a distinguished member of the Royal Navy and went rogue. Others, believe that he was a pirate himself. No one knows the truth, only that he had in his possession a map which brought him here. Well, there." She points toward the fort.

"The Metairie Stronghold," I say, recalling the plat I'd looked at earlier while with the lawyer.

"Along with two other guys—"

"Friends or foes?"

"Both? Jeb Dubois, Roger Cahoot, and Tickle called themselves the Boot Beer Boys, "

"Let me guess, this was during prohibition."

She nods. "However, on account of the abundance of sassafras, Tickle brewed root beer. He also gambled. Anyway, they discovered what we call the Dubois Diamond and the Roger Cahoot Ruby."

"That's three guys. Two treasures. Was there a falling out?"

"It's pure speculation, but supposedly there was a third stone or treasure. Again, no one knows for sure, but they'll all claim they do."

I lean in, rapt by Honey's sweet yet smokey voice as if we're gathered around a campfire and she's telling old tales. "What do you think?"

"I figured you'd know considering you're supposedly Tickle's kin and all." She clicks her tongue.

I shake my head. "No relation. As I said, I came into this inheritance in my divorce settlement."

"What did *she* end up with?"

My lips bunch up with a shameful amount of self-satisfaction. "Nothing. Not even an ounce of my regret. I won't let myself remember so much as her name."

"Never mind a woman scorned ..." Honey mutters.

"If withholding my forgiveness was worthwhile, trust me, I'd do it."

"So you forgave her?"

I nod, just barely. However, I'll never forget.

Honey golf claps. "Yet you're here and you're not the first person to come through, claiming the property. Though this approach is new. Well done. As it is, my sleep is spotty and you'd have had to get up mighty early in the morning to pull one over on me."

I sputter. "Wait? You don't believe me?"

"Remember where you are. This is Hogwash. Ground Zero for nonsense."

"Honey, I have the documents to prove it to you."

"Papers can be forged."

"You say that like you have experience."

She chortles.

"If you think this is a scam, why are you out here with me? Or are you just seeing how far I can be strung along?" Like Molly sweeping up whatever crumbs of gossip she can, is Honey gathering information about the treasure? Granted, I'd heard vaguely about it when the town came into my possession, but I didn't believe it. As she stated, this town is called Hogwash.

With a dismissive snort, she gestures to the tomb. "Why don't we pay our respects."

I study the writing on the grave marker and read, "'When Pigs Fly.'"

"It's kind of the town slogan," Honey says.

I read the next line, "'I would just as soon imbibe this root as take to the air and make a hoot. Look up and see me on the blocks, the blocks made of pinkish rocks. You'll find me sketched there, most rectangular seldom square.' What does that mean?"

"By my reckoning, the best people to ask about the first riddle would be Lexi and JQ, but that doesn't mean they'll answer you."

"This seems like a bunch of gibberish." Before Honey can remind me again that we're in Hogwash, I read the next one. "'Take one from apple but none from tart. Find one in liver but not in heart. The last you'll discover in giant as well as ghost but never, ever in a roast.'"

Honey hugs her arms around her chest. Without the sun, it's cooling off. If I had a hoodie, I'd offer it. But I'm not sure her shiver is because she's chilly.

"What did Hogan Tickle mean by these riddles?"

"Legends have grown up over the years, but one thing is for sure, instead of leaving his fortune to his son, he cut Sebastien out of the will. These are the only clues to his inheritance."

"So there's more to it than the chateau?"

Honey's arms shift from a hug to crossed in front of her chest and she levels me with a sharp and accusatory look. "I figured that's why you're here."

I shake my head slowly.

"People have tried to solve the riddles because supposedly they lead to Tickle's Golden Tokens, which would then bring them to the treasure. A bunch of scavenger hunters really, every year descending on Hogwash, making a mess of things and thinking that if they find an owl, an apple, or a pig, that'll lead them to a fortune."

"But no one has ever solved a riddle or found a token?"

"Some say it's cursed."

"That isn't a direct answer."

She remains tight-lipped.

"Any idea what happened to the other Boot Beer Boys?"

"One was hung. Another died in a duel. Supposedly."

"And their treasures?"

"I've heard that the diamond was chipped into pieces and sold—the Swans had a chunk. As for the ruby, no one knows."

I read the last three riddles in my head, trying to make sense of them.

*I have a head and a tail. I can break, but I am not frail. If you feed me, I will plink, but don't you worry, I do not stink.*

I chuckle.

"Everyone thinks that has something to do with a skunk."

"You have your doubts."

"If there was a treasure, trust me, it would've been found."

"You sound confident."

"More like convicted."

"In the court of law?"

"Something like that," she mutters, shivering again.

The next one reads, *You can hold me tight but not to cuddle. However, I prefer the muddle minus three especially if there's a puddle. I cannot sew or sow, but I am the latter and getting fatter.*

The final one says, *The story is that of the three, one lives in a house made of a tree. The other you could blow over, but not mine even though it's in a field of clover.*

My gaze trails back up the list of riddles and lands on the

second one before drifting over to Honey who watches me intently. My pulse trips.

She says, "You inherited this place. Shouldn't you know its history?"

"Probably better to hear it from a local." This local, in particular, with her smoky voice, as sweet as honey and as crackly as a campfire.

I tell myself I'm not looking—not at her brown eyes filled with secrets or her full lips covered in promise. Nor am I looking for the treasure, but if I found it, I wouldn't complain.

Shrouded in the silence of twilight, we make our way back to the truck.

Once inside, I ask, "So what do you think?"

"About the treasure? I say don't put any stock in false hopes. Foolish ones. They've been the doom of many people."

"Dramatic."

"I think living a quiet life, a simple one is the best course of action."

"Says the woman who has a Porsche in her garage."

She snorts a breath. "It's more of a carport, er, a tarp strung up between two trees, a broken laundry drying pole, and a broom handle."

"You should have a car like that in a garage."

"I'm well aware. As it is, I'm not in possession of a garage. I'm lucky I have a roof."

"I have a garage."

She pumps her hand in the air. "Well done. You succeeded at life."

I gesture over my shoulder toward the chateau. "I have a proposal. Help me fix up the place. You can park your Porsche there and make me flapjacks."

"I don't see how that works in my favor. Also, they're called pancakes."

I chuckle. Having scrapped the plan that brought me to town this morning, a new one takes an amorphous shape. I'm not sure what it'll look like in the end, but I want Honey to be part of it. Show her that life isn't all briars and bramble. I'll have to reformulate my revenge plot later.

I say, "You have a vision for what it once was."

"There are old photos on the wall in the town hall. An entire book in the library. More of a scrapbook, but Friends of Hogwash preserved what they could."

I idle at the end of the overgrown road that intersects Main Street.

"Maybe I want your help."

"And how would that benefit me?"

"You said you're lucky you have a roof. When the chateau is restored, you can live there."

Her laugh is robust then cuts off abruptly. "Why would you let me do that?"

"Because you have every reason to leave this town, yet you haven't. Something keeps you here."

"I'm beholden." Her voice is faint then louder when she adds, "As it is, I can't stack more onto my plate. And I don't mean pancakes because there's no such thing as too many pancakes, but there is such a thing as too much work ..."

"Flapjacks."

Her phone beeps a few times. She checks the text. "I have to get back. Now."

"So long as no one tries to take my parking spot, I'll have you to the Laughing Gator Grille in less than sixty seconds. By the way, any recommendations for lodging?"

Her fingers fly across her phone's screen as she replies to a text while saying, "There's the Pigs in a Blanket B&B."

"Huggers really go all out with the theme, huh?"

She rolls her eyes. "Hoggers."

"Sounds to me like you're saying Huggers."

"Anyway, I don't think Thelma will let you stay. At least not yet. She's wary of outsiders and only allows locals, though Jesse recently moved out, so I know there's space. Why not stay at the chateau, unless you're scared." The corner of her mouth curls with a smile.

"I'll figure it out. Good luck trying to get rid of me."

"And good luck sleeping at the chateau. Watch out for swamp zombies." She laughs as she gets out of the truck in front of the restaurant and hurries inside.

Lexi and a man sit at the counter. She holds a baby and Honey lights up.

I can't say I'm particularly afraid of ghosts, swamp zombies, or even the crocogator, but babies terrify me because they operate on their own principles. On the flight here, an infant wailed for a solid forty-five minutes. I know they don't come with an off switch, but how can a guy who's used to turning off alarms, not feel helpless in that situation—and, let's be real, somewhat annoyed?

But what frightens me even more is the way Honey Hamilton messes with my pulse.

# Chapter 7

## *Then Comes the Baby in the Baby Carriage*

After the ever so rude interruption of Maddock in his monster truck, I resume my normal routine for the next week: evening feedings and stories with Leonie and sunny autumn mornings where I forget about how the little beastie woke me up numerous times throughout the night. All I can think about is her happy smile, serving coffee and pancakes with the best smile I can muster, rinse and repeat.

I hardly think about Maddock except when the roll-off dumpster service trucks drives past, hauling away load after load from the Tickle estate. An equal number of work trucks go the other way with signage for electricians, plumbers, and carpenters.

I hardly notice him when he enters and exits the Coffee Loft across the street, wearing work boots and a flannel. His stubble makes him look rugged. There must not be a mirror in the chateau.

Not that he needs to look in one to know he's handsome.

Not that I think that.

But I'm looking in the mirror right now, wondering if that

line next to my left eye used to be there. Pfft. Pageant queen? More like pancake queen and I don't mind.

Not much.

Though sometimes, I wouldn't mind having someone ... you know, a special person. One I could ask about is whether this wrinkle makes me look old or if this skirt makes my butt look big. I already know the answers, but would it be so bad for someone to love me so much that they'd tell me I'm beautiful? To love me despite the imperfections?

Leonie lets out a roar from her spot, bolstered on the bed. I playfully pounce, giving her tickles and nuzzles. She's the sweetest little pea and I'm lucky that she landed on my doorstep.

She simultaneously helps me forget the stack of unopened bills, the letters from my mother, and the little itch in the back of my mind that so desperately wants to be scratched.

"Not today, Maddock," I singsong to Leonie even though she has no idea what I'm saying ... and I have no idea how I'm feeling other than conflicted about how much I liked when his gaze strayed to me ... and the pit of disappointment inside when it didn't.

To distract myself, I do the "This Little Piggy" song while gently pinching my little girl's toes. Content for a moment, I pack up her diaper bag for the day. My phone buzzes and I read the message from Mara. All three of her kids have the stomach bug. That means no sitter today.

"Since they don't make hazmat suits that fit five-month-olds, it's take your daughter to work day," I say to Leonie, trying to muster up enthusiasm.

My shoulders sink, but I tell myself I can conquer this single motherhood gig without succumbing to illegal activities. Sure, it's all I know, but there is another way. A better way than my mother's role modeling.

I won't land in jail, leaving Leonie to fend for herself.

But today will require some creativity of the not-illegal sort.

My single-wide isn't far from the Laughing Gator Grille, but I need to bring reinforcements, so I pack the Porsche full of baby accouterments, including her swing, jumper, activity mat, and bouncer.

Then I call in backup.

Molly eyes my red Porsche Spyder. It's among the top ten fastest models ever made and there's no way she's getting behind the wheel. I rarely do these days.

Yes, I trust her more with the baby. Leonie is nestled safely in her stroller. I will not be held responsible if Molly runs over Mrs. Halfpenny's "dog," Frodo.

While I review the rules, her phone beeps incessantly.

She says, "I accept payment on my new app: PayMo."

"My flip phone doesn't host apps."

She bunches up her lips. "Will you make me cream brool?"

I huff. "Yes. Fine. I'll make you crème brûlée. But this is the last time. Eggs are getting expensive."

"And so am I," Molly sasses back.

"Well, if Chick Jagger would do his job, maybe your hens would start producing more chicks you could open a farm stand."

She looks from side to side. "Um, the mayor is in meetings out of town."

"Your rooster is in meetings out of town?"

"He has important assemblies and summits to attend." Her phone beeps again.

"You don't know where he is, do you?"

"It's not like I'm his assistant. He has business to take care of. So do we. Are we going to the Grille or not?" Her phone rings this time. No doubt, it's Roxanne.

I point to her device. "Check that now. No talking or texting while walking."

"Okay, sidewalk police," she mutters. The call goes to voicemail, but Molly reviews the messages. Her eyes light up with the kind of fervor that tells me she just got some juicy gossip.

"Um, I've gotta go. Sorry. I'll take a rain check on the cream brool."

"But you didn't even help me."

"It's early. You interrupted my beauty sleep." She dashes off, phone to her ear.

I rock back, wondering how I'm going to get myself, the baby, and all her gear to the restaurant. I've already cut back the weekend hours. The Coffee Klatch—or Klatch for short, what the group of old timers call themselves even though they drink sweet tea—who camp out and complain about low crop yields and weevils weren't too pleased about that. But it's Wednesday and the guys are going to be lined up and cantankerous if the front door isn't unlocked in ten minutes.

"Who else can I call?" I zip through my mental list of contacts.

A truck rolls by with out-of-state plates. The taillights glow and the rise and fall of a tinny voice comes through the vehicle's sound system, rude during this early hour.

No surprise, it's Maddock and he must be on a call. During the Hogwash Hunt, cars stop at the entrance to Sunnyside Mobile Home Park & Campground all the time because the cell service drops off on the Tickle property and beyond.

I start pushing the stroller toward the truck and then stop. Nope. I'm not going to bother him. He's busy.

Turning back, I tell myself I'll return for Leonie's stuff later. She'll be content in the stroller for a little while.

On cue, she fusses. One of her socks is missing. Of course. I tickle her foot, earning a little laugh, and replace the sock.

Making a U-turn with the stroller, I approach Maddock's truck as his voice booms through the speaker. Sounds like an important call.

"Never mind. We'll find another way." I'm about to turn around again, when the unmistakable sound of a power window lowers, followed by him calling, "Honey!"

I freeze. Been caught. Leonie's little face wrinkles, the precursor to a cry. This is her active time and she's been in the stroller too long without movement or stimulation.

Biting my lip, I raise my hand with a slight wave—the kind you give a neighbor when you can't, or don't want to, stop to talk.

"What are you doing here?" he asks from on high in his fancy truck.

"I live here." And I'm not ashamed, despite what Jesse said about me belonging on Marais Way. It's not even one of my dreams. I'd be satisfied with plumbing that doesn't leak.

He looks around, expression mild.

"Early for a walk. The sun is hardly up."

"On my way to work."

He peers into the carriage. "With a baby?"

I shift from foot to foot, not wanting to explain my predicament. Yes, I need a family-friendly car. But since I'm stuck with the Porsche until Leonie is old enough to safely and legally sit in the two-seater, it's travel by foot or borrow a vehicle.

Just then, Leonie decides to roar her into the conversation.

Maddock does the one thing I don't want him to do. He opens the truck's door and approaches us. His close-cropped brown hair is clean like he cares. He wears faded denim jeans and a flannel over a T-shirt as if he wants to seem like he doesn't care that much.

"What do we have here?" He approaches cautiously like one would an actual lioness and her cub.

"This is Leonie."

Face contorted as if he's afraid he might catch cooties, Maddock cranes his neck. "She has pipes."

"Yes, and she's about to wake up the neighborhood. No one wants Mrs. Halfpenny's dog barking at this hour." I gently rock the stroller to soothe the baby.

"She doesn't turn off at night?"

"Are you talking about the baby or the dog?"

He chuckles.

I quickly explain that the deputy sheriff gets a panicked call once a month from Mrs. Halfpenny and has to surreptitiously change out Frodo's triple-As.

Maddock runs his hand through his hair. "Only in Hugwash Holler."

"Hogwash," I correct as the sun peeks through the buildings in the east, meaning the clock is ticking—on Leonie and the opening hour.

"I still say that it sounds to me like you're saying Hugwash."

I can practically see the Klatch fuming from here. "Sounds to me like you're not going to get pancakes today."

He pumps his hands. "Are you this sassy because you woke up on the wrong side of the bed or is it because you haven't yet had coffee?"

Despite my threat, I can't afford to turn away business. I shoot him a sharp glare and expect one in return. Instead, he wears a smirky, smoldery smile as if he's figuring out what makes me tick.

Relenting, I say, "Will you help me?"

His eyebrow arches and his eyes dart from the Coffee Loft down the street to my house.

"I mean with the baby." The request comes out of desperation with Leonie having already pulled the pin on her itty bitty baby grenade and the Klatch being a reliable source of a daily twenty dollars.

We already had a falling out once over me being too headstrong and stubborn for my own good. Mrs. Daley more or less made things right. I'm on thin ice as it is with the Klatch.

Maddock's eyes widen. "You want my help? What's the magic word?"

"Never mind."

Leonie doesn't like this and starts wailing. Forgetting about Maddock, I coo and coddle her until she decommissions the nuclear event.

He slowly backs away. Good. I don't need his help. But as the sun reflects off the Porsche, I'm reminded that I really, really do.

Turning around, I call, "Please, will you help me?"

He halts, hand on the door of the truck. His eyes land on me and with the way the early morning sun glows, I almost trick myself into thinking they spark.

"Can you please push the stroller to the restaurant?"

He straightens. "Uh. Yeah. No. Probably not. I'm not equipped."

"It's right there." I point.

"Looks like you have a line forming at the front door already."

I continue to gently rock Leonie in the carriage. "Exactly. You have long legs. It'll take you two minutes tops to get there."

"What if she starts crying again?" He steps closer, gazing at the baby as if assessing a digital clock counting down to detonation.

"I'll be there waiting for you," I assure him.

"I take it you're going to drive over there?" He eyes the Porsche.

"Yes. I have a bunch of stuff to bring. That way, I can open, pour the Klatch their sweet tea, and get everything set up for her. So will you?" Desperate now, I tip my head toward the carriage.

"How about I drive," he says.

"Um, my vehicle isn't exactly street-legal." I cough-whisper the last part.

He raises an eyebrow. "I see."

"You neither saw nor heard anything."

He lets out a long breath as if resigning himself to helping me.

The sun dapples the top of the stroller and I pull the little shade up so it doesn't get in her eyes. This brings with it a cascade of dangling toys and she lets out a happy coo.

"She's content. Will you please push her there?"

Maddock pockets his keys, looks around as if checking to make sure no one is about to witness this, and rolls his fingers as he grips the stroller's handlebar.

My lips ripple with amusement. "Is a big bad firefighter like you afraid of a baby?"

He tucks his chin. "What? No?"

I sense a question in his voice.

She kicks her feet, sending a sock sailing. I stash it in the cupholder for now.

I clap him on the back. "You can do this."

"Yeah, of course. Duh. No big deal."

It sounds like he's talking himself into it, which doesn't give me a lot of confidence.

Drawing a deep breath to drum up some of my own, I say, "This is how it's going to work. I'm going to drive a quarter of a mile to the restaurant. You're going to push Leonie, sing nursery rhymes, and enjoy it." And hopefully, our deputy sheriff will continue to look the other way if he runs my plates and sees that my registration is expired.

It's not because I defy the law. More like I don't have the cash to pay the fees.

Squinting, Maddock asks, "What's in it for me?"

"Aside from spending time with my adorable baby?"

He wrinkles his nose. "Babies smell."

"They smell amazing like—" But there are no words to describe Leonie's sweet baby scent.

He wrinkles his nose as if to remind me about dirty diapers.

"Most of the time," I mutter, recalling the close call last week in Missy's Corolla.

Looking down the street, Maddock seems to measure the distance. I'm running out of time. The Klatch will either riot and break the Grille's windows or call in a wellness check, which will unnecessarily bring Jesse into the situation. He's already overlooked the fact that my vehicle's registration is expired and we won't discuss the lapsed insurance policy. That's a problem for another day.

"Look both ways when you cross the street. Watch for cracks in the sidewalk." I'm suddenly nervous about Maddock pushing the carriage.

"Exactly how much time do you spend in Hogwash?" he asks.

My meeting out of town the first time I'd left in a month. I point to the farm road to our left and Shady Lane, the slightly less overgrown road that leads to the Tickle estate and beyond, to my right. "There's a road right there and you never know what kind of beast mobile might come barreling down here."

He lets out a slightly annoyed breath.

I smile. "Obey the speed limits."

He shakes his head slightly and sets off, pushing the stroller. Ignoring how I'm inexplicably attracted to this man, like a race day, I spring into action, sliding behind the wheel like the pro I used to be. Maddock and Leonie are only halfway to the restaurant by the time I get there. That might be a record other than the time Mrs. Halfpenny called to tell me someone was on the restaurant's roof. Turns out it was Chick Jagger. Now that I think of it, that was the last time we saw the mayor. Don't worry, I ushered him down to safety.

Once parked, I wave my hands, okay, flail like there's a fire, as I rush toward the Klatch. "I'm coming."

Hank grunts. "I was starting to consider heading over to the Coffee Loft."

"They don't sell sweet tea," I say, ushering them inside.

"They don't have a counter like this either," Dick says, thankfully on my side.

Buck adds, "But Tallula always opens on time."

"It won't happen again," I say as Maddock and the carriage come into view.

I could carry out the duties of opening this place in my sleep—I did once, early on when Leonie came into my care, and I hadn't gotten used to the late-night interruptions. Everything is on and operational, mostly, when I hear Antoine's old Plymouth rumble into the rear lot.

Clapping my hands, the old timers proceed with their klatching and I hold open the door for the stroller which Maddock pushes like he's on the wrong side of a steamroller. Leonie wails and I scoop her up, wave Maddock off, and flip on the grill at the same time, Antoine asks, "Where's the fire? I just saw the firefighter run down the street."

"Running away is more like it. He might be afraid of babies. Or allergic. I didn't ask."

Antoine chuckles and takes Leonie, bouncing her. The guy has five kids, which includes a set of twins, so I don't give him the baby safety spiel.

His two-minute morning greeting with her affords me time to get all of Leonie's gear from the car. I'm panting and out of breath all morning, but the rest of the day is me rotating her from my arms to the various hand-me-down bouncers, saucers, and baby activity centers I've set up behind the counter, making it so I have to pass through an obstacle course when Mr. Soto comes in for his afternoon milkshake.

By the time Antoine shuts off the grill and says goodbye, I contemplate spending the night right here. My feet ache, my hair frizzes, and I'm frazzled, but the baby is as animated as ever.

At least she's not crying.

"We made it." I rub my dry eyes. "Survived the day."

Then the door jingles. I forgot to lock it and turn off the bright overhead lights and flip over the *Open* sign. Maybe I can fire up the restaurant in my sleep, but not shut it down for the day ... at least not while looking after a baby.

"We're closed," I call.

Footsteps approach.

I pop up and nearly collide with Maddock who's peering over the counter.

He's tall, but so am I. Still, I have to lift my gaze to meet his eyes. It's like he wishes he could tower over me. Maddock is the kind of guy who's used to being in charge and having women tripping over him.

Well, not this woman. Instead, I'm flipping and flapping over him, which I still can't quite explain, but the twitchiness inside just won't quit.

# Chapter 8

## *Dinner for Deux*

**B**abies freak me out. Terrify me. They're loud but fragile. Demanding yet can't explain what they want. Plus, they leak snot and pee and poop and ooze mysterious stickiness.

Not having kids was one thing my ex and I agreed on. For my part, mostly because I was told I probably wouldn't be able to.

Compared to Honey who is self-sufficient, Emberly was needy, loud, and secretive given the fact that I had no idea she was the heiress of a town.

I tell myself to ignore the flames inside when I think about Honey or when I'm around her. I just barely got out of a marriage alive.

But maybe I want her to want me a little. Perhaps I like that she asked for my help this morning.

I don't know how I survived pushing the infant in a stroller to the restaurant. At least it wasn't raining. Right now, the drizzle is light, but the winds are heavy. Earlier, I saw on the forecast there's a storm in the Gulf, but the meteorologists predict it'll blow itself out before it gets here.

The work on the chateau today built up an appetite. Specifically, a hankering for flapjacks ... and maybe seeing Honey again. She occupies my thoughts when she shouldn't. Her honeysuckle scent fills the air even though I've been working in the moldering chateau all day.

Here I am, doing the opposite of what I promised myself. Not doing what I usually do. Feeling how I usually feel. Should feel.

Honey said she's single. I can't imagine her being a single mom, because only a loser would leave her and she doesn't seem the type to tolerate losers. I figured she must've been babysitting and mixed up the schedule or was helping someone out in a pinch. But maybe I was wrong.

A few loose strands of her wildflower honey-blonde hair hang in her face. She blows them out of the way and unties her apron. "We're closed."

"You're here."

"I'm cleaning up."

"Looks like you're playing with the baby."

"How could I not? She's adorable." Honey glances at the little one with affection in her eyes.

"I'm hungry."

"You've been filling up on beignets." She narrows her eyes at me as if I committed treachery.

The baby lets out a shriek.

Honey winds up a dial on one of the toys and what sounds like a drunk clown sings while plastic boxes light up with a rainbow of colors.

"The muffins over there are pretty good."

"Traitor," she says with a slight laugh like she's torn

between wanting to serve me flapjacks and banning me from the restaurant altogether.

The sound ignites the pilot light inside me—I hadn't realized it had gone out. At times, Honey's laughter can be smoky, flirty, or a tease—a taste promising more. She laughs easily, usually robustly, even though it doesn't seem like her life is easy. To most people in her shoes, it wouldn't seem like much is funny.

But I cannot get enough of the sound.

This past week, I've seen her, Mara, the Coffee Loft owner, and her sister Tallula standing in the street talking, so if they're rivals, they're especially friendly ones. And yeah, Honey was wearing a sweater dress with tall boots and had her hair up off her neck one of the times. Another, she had on a crew neck sweatshirt and shorts which revealed a bit more of her long legs than the skirts she normally wears, like the one she has on now. It has a tie around the waist and swishes when she walks. Her fitted shirt has a tiny tear by her shoulder.

Around a yawn, she says, "I used to serve grilled muffins."

"How about flapjacks?"

"Now? It's nearly dinnertime."

The idea of having dinner together floats into my mind and melts like hot butter on a griddle. "Haven't you ever had breakfast for dinner?"

It's then I realize that since I walked in, she's been in motion—flipping the *Open* sign over, dimming the lights, refilling things. "I'm lucky if I ever sit down and eat."

"Maybe we should do something about that. So no flapjacks?"

She parts her lips as if she's going to correct me, but instead says, "Come back tomorrow."

"Are you inviting me to return to this fine establishment?"

The huff I expect is more like a *druff*, a droopy huff—the

kind that comes from exhaustion. "If by fine, you mean I pass the season health code inspections, then sure."

The Laughing Gator Grille has a frozen-in-time look with paneled walls, seventies wallpaper print, and lots of alligator kitsch. I hadn't noticed the first time I came in ... because my attention was elsewhere. My pulse does something weird, and I realize that was mostly because I'd been captivated by the woman behind the counter.

She comes out from behind it now and marches over to the door as if to show me out.

I hesitate. "Well, for the favor I did, you owe me cream brool, at least."

Honey doesn't flash the smile I'd hoped for. "I know that you know it's pronounced crème brûlée."

"I was just joking." My stomach growls.

As if unable to turn away someone hungry, Honey says, "I have some leftover boudin." She pronounces it, *boo dan.*

"I'm not convinced the estate is ghost-free. Maybe I should leave them some *boo* dan."

The baby laughs or screeches, I'm not sure.

"Boudin is sausage made with pork, onions, garlic, and some other stuff."

"Secret stuff?"

"Everyone knows most of my recipes include honey, so it's not like a secret ingredient."

I can't help but think she has some secrets.

"There's also some leftover potato salad that I was going to put on special tomorrow."

"Can I take it to-go?"

She is already boxing it up.

"Actually, can you make it a double portion?"

"Magic word?"

The corner of my mouth tugs with a smile, recalling our

exchange this morning. "Please." I hesitate, then add, "Will you join me?"

"For what?"

"Dinner?"

Her hands flap and she drops the lid to the takeout container. "Me?"

The baby fusses, goes quiet, then turns red before a rumble comes from behind the counter.

Honey's eyes widen.

The baby wails.

Flustered, she turns in a circle.

I'm equipped to deal with advancing hose lines, navigating smoky environments, and handling hazardous materials. I've rescued cats from trees and used the jaws of life more times than I'd like. But I'm not sure how to save Honey from this situation.

Looking like she's running on empty, she starts to remove the baby from the complicated safety straps in the little seat with bells, whistles, and all kinds of gadgets, but her hands shake.

When she said she rarely sits down to eat, I think I now understand why ... and have my doubts she's consumed much of anything today.

If only I had on my protective gear. All the same, I run into the flames of Honey's life.

I carefully unlatch the harness clips. The baby's little fingers wrap around my thumb as she kicks wildly with only one sock on.

"Maddock, I got—" Honey starts.

But the little one is already snug in my arms and goes quiet. Her hands are now in fists and her eyes are screwed shut, but she's calmer.

"Magic word, magic touch. I've got it all."

Honey lifts her arm to playfully swat me but must be too tired.

"Come on. We'll go over to the house and have something to eat." My nose twitches and my appetite disappears as a foul odor wafts ...

Her lip teases a knowing smile. "You sure you got it?"

"Maybe I'll leave diaper duty to you." Holding the baby away from me, her feet kick while she chews on her hand.

Honey expertly takes Leonie into her arms and they disappear down the hallway to the bathroom. The faint sound of singing filters toward me.

My mother wasn't a singer, but she did hum. Strange to think that the Witt line ends with me. I don't have siblings and I probably won't ever have kids—if the doctors' warnings were on target, I probably can't.

Honey returns with a clean and quiet Leonie. They both look exhausted. The latter from the tough life of a baby, what with the eating, sleeping, and constant attention from being so demandingly adorable. And the former, well, from trying to look after said baby while running a restaurant.

Despite Honey's sassiness, there's something undeniably admirable about her taking care of Leonie with so much love and dedication. Her life isn't just her own and I don't think that kind of humility, purpose, and sense of duty can come from anything other than parenthood.

It makes her glow in a way that I can't quite explain.

Plus, she looks really great in that skirt.

But while she's taking care of the baby, who's taking care of her? I want Honey to eat the *boo dan* and potato salad while seated. Thankfully, I have a table—a huge one.

I pick up two of the baby items and start toward the front door.

"What are you doing?"

"Taking you home," I call over my shoulder as I head outside into the rain.

"Maddock, I can—"

I turn around and look pointedly at the stroller, reminding Honey of this morning's adventure.

Two minutes later, the bed of the truck is loaded with the baby's gear. I roll the cover out to keep it dry from the rain and the stroller basket is strapped safely in the rear seat.

It's a one-minute ride to the mobile home park, but I bypass it and continue down the dark road that leads to the estate. The trees above block the rain and the windshield wipers squeak.

"I'd like to argue with you about our destination, but—" Honey starts.

"But you're tired, which is why we're going here first."

When the headlights sweep the old estate, glowing from inside, Honey sits up.

I'm under a bit of pressure from Leyton to decide on whether I'm going to take up his offer, so I pulled out all the stops to get this place cleaned up before I decide what to do.

"Wow. It's transformed." Her mouth hangs open.

I hired a crew to clear away all the overgrowth and under-growth surrounding the exterior. I think letting in a little sunshine might sanitize the place. While they were at work, along with a few guys from town—the ones Honey calls the Klatch—we cleared out all the junk inside. Over the weekend, I hired a house cleaning service to scrub, wipe, and clean the grime.

"It's not about to get the white glove treatment and there's still a ton of work to do, but I think health services and the parish building inspector took the chateau off the top of the list for places to condemn."

Hunched against the rain, I jog to the passenger side and

open the door and then take out the stroller basket containing the baby. It's surprisingly heavy.

Walking up the front steps, Honey says, "It's remarkable what a week can do."

"And several thousand dollars worth of excavation equipment, Dumpsters, and elbow grease. I figured I'd start on the outside."

"And the inside?" she asks as we enter the chateau.

"Mostly just cleaning. I had a crew here along with several contractors to assess what I'm dealing with."

"I'll admit that I'm impressed."

"This brings me back to my request ..."

Honey shifts her weight, and the baby lets out a little coo.

"Can I warm up her food first?" Honey is a blur in the kitchen as she does I-don't-know-what with a pot of hot water and a baby bottle. Thankfully, the stove burners work. Moments later, Leonie makes a purring sound as she drinks warm milk. She droops and drifts in Honey's arms. After a little hiccup, her eyes close and she falls asleep.

With the baby safely in the stroller basket, I set out the containers from the Laughing Gator Grille.

I gesture to the chair. "Sit."

Despite the exhaustion etched on her features, Honey shoots me a glare.

"Please sit."

She eyes the chair like it's a dangerous object as if she uses it, she may never get up again. Getting to my feet, I pull it out and then wait until she lowers down.

After a prayer, Honey digs into the meal like a lioness and her kill.

"You didn't eat all day, did you?"

Around a mouthful, she says, "No time."

"Even when it was slow?"

"I was busy—orders, paperwork, preparing sides, baking. I wear all the hats, except chef most days. And of course, keeping this one from having a meltdown." She tucks the blanket into the side of the basket.

"Is she yours?" I ask, oddly worried about the answer. Not because that would make Honey a mother, but because there was once someone in her life she loved enough to share a life with and all the flirting, smiles, and memories that come with that. Yet, he's not here which means someone got hurt.

Honey sets down her fork. "Is she my baby? Technically, yes. Biologically, no."

"I thought you were babysitting. At least, at first."

Leonie lets out a wail and Honey launches to her feet. The woman is definitely a mom. Resting the baby on her shoulder, she bounces slightly and gently taps her back. "That's it. You just need to burp."

After a few minutes of this, Leonie lets out a man-sized belch. Then she nestles down in the crook of Honey's neck.

She closes her eyes and wavers on her feet. "Ooh. I have to go."

I guide her to the chair and notice the spit-up dribbling down her back.

"I'll get you a shirt."

"Maddock, I'm used to this. You don't have to—"

But I'm already in the other room, rooting through my clean laundry until I find a Reno FD T-shirt.

When I return, Honey says, "As I said, I come with strings attached."

I try to take the baby from her arms, but she has her pudgy little fingers wrapped in Honey's hair. I gently peel them loose. Making contact with her silky hair sends a jolt straight into my heart. My breath catches and I stagger slightly. Thankfully, Honey is too tired to notice.

Like I'm handling a live bomb, I carefully take the baby out of Honey's arms and tell her where the bathroom is so she can clean up and change.

"I know where it is," she murmurs.

Leonie nuzzles against me. Her sweet baby scent tickles my nose. I tug my shirt up a bit on my neck. I need to shave and don't want her soft little head rubbing against my sandpaper stubble.

Her little fists relax and she becomes a baby blob in my arms. Completely at ease, safe and secure.

Honey returns, wearing my gray shirt. It's oversized and grazes her thighs. I swallow thickly and cannot tear my gaze away.

She says, "Maybe you do have the magic touch. So far, only ladies have been able to soothe her, which was a bit of a problem since our caseworker was a guy."

I don't imagine the fine lines around Honey's eyes were there a few months ago. Even though some of them likely resulted from fatigue and stress, I imagine more came from smiling the way she does now as she pats Leonie's rump.

She says, "Let me take her so you can finish eating."

I shake my head. "Nah. You eat first."

"No, seriously. I'll eat later."

"Honey." My voice is stern because I eat most of my meals seated and at a regular pace. Plus, I don't want to disturb the baby ... and I rather like the idea that she's content in my arms "Please eat."

"You're so bossy."

"And you're so sassy."

"So what does that make us?" she asks.

That makes us the worst or best match ever.

# Chapter 9

## *Hurrican Hogan*

Buck says, "That last one wasn't worthy of a name. I think they jumped the gun givin' this one a moniker."

"That's because it's your name," Dick says, finishing his glass of sweet tea.

Hank asks, "Buck's name isn't Buck?"

It's hard for my ears not to twitch at this information. Granted, it's not Molly and Pest Digest-level gossip, but up until I was twenty-three years old, I knew Buck as Mr. Daley. I couldn't conceive of the old farmer having a first name, no less it not being Buck.

Dick chuckles. "Head on over to the library. I think they have the old school yearbooks stashed somewhere."

I inwardly groan. I hope that's not true. My hair was about a mile high thanks to Betsy and Mama. To this day, I still call the former Miss Betsy.

Despite what Maddock might think, I do have manners ... and am not always sassy.

As I put away the clean coffee mugs, I go still.

What is he doing back here?

Well, not here *here*. But in my head.

"I charge rent, you know," I murmur.

"What's that?" Hank asks.

"Oh, nothing. Just talking to myself." Which is a new habit, along with thinking about Maddock. A habit I want to kick, thank you very much. I root around in the wooden drawer under the cash register for a lollipop.

"Let me guess," Hank says. "Is it Wilbur? Elrod? Applesauce?"

"Ain't no one who'd name their kid applesauce," Buck fires back.

"I have an aunt Peaches," Dick says.

They all laugh.

If I had more time on my hands, I'd get to the bottom of this. Across the street, Thelma locks up the Hogwash Hairwash early. She must be hunkering down for this storm that has the guys speculating about whether it'll be named. The last one missed us—the night I went to Tickle's estate and had dinner with Maddock.

That night, the baby spit-up didn't make me bat an eyelash. No, my cheeks flushed for another reason. When I walked into the dining room wearing the fire department T-shirt, the way Maddock looked at me with longing gave me a full-body flush. And the way *he* looked all massive with broad shoulders and big hands holding Leonie took my breath away.

Or it could've been the ghosts haunting the old house. That's what I keep telling myself.

"Ouch."

The Klatch trio goes quiet and looks my way.

"Bumped into the pie case," I mutter.

The wooden one that has been there all my life. The one that I can navigate around while holding six luncheon special plates or a tray full of large cups filled with sweet tea. Yeah, that one. The solid one that reminds me that ghosts aren't real.

But the way my thoughts repeatedly loop back to Maddock like I'm doing laps on a race track is very much real.

I sigh.

"All the same, I say you haul in the last of that crop in case the field floods, Buck ... if that's your real name," Hank says.

"I've been Buck since I was old enough to answer my mama and that's what you're going to call me no matter what the yearbook says."

I stifle a laugh. If nothing else, these guys keep me entertained. Well, the twenty dollars they leave me for occupying the counter for several hours each day and keeping my sweet tea the freshest in Cameron Parish helps, too.

It's nearly November, which is late in storm season, so I'm guessing this one will bypass us, too. Hogwash residents used to have big storm parties, with everyone gathering at the largest homes or the community center. Funny that it could survive an atom bomb attack, but the swamp has just about reclaimed it. Then again, I did see a parish truck over there the other day, probably assessing how to best demolish it.

While Molly, with her loud mouth, broadcasts everyone's business in town, I notice everything but keep my mouth shut—okay, maybe my lips are parted a little bit. Through the window, Maddock looks good this morning in dark jeans and a fitted flannel with thick hair that's freshly trimmed—he must be coming from the salon. But he doesn't cross the street. Instead, he struts into the Coffee Loft.

I stick my tongue out. "Traitor. Tallula is the real beauty queen in town. Sorry, Maddock, she's taken. She and our sheriff are newly hitched."

All three guys at the counter stare at me.

I realize I spoke all of that out loud.

"I'll just go write the lunch special on the board now."

Dick shakes his head. "Honey, I don't like what I'm seeing to the east. I reckon you should close early today. Go home, kick up your feet, and watch the rain not rip off your roof."

Last year, before Leonie came along, after a particularly wet fall, I came home to a tree branch, a nest, and a mama bird in my living room. Thankfully, my books were spared and not a soggy mess. At the time, second to the Porsche, the contents of my bookshelves were my most prized possessions—I should probably return a few of the first editions to the chateau's library. Mama said to help myself, so I did, by learning all about ancient world history right up to the founding of this country. The lesson is history repeats itself and wisdom can prevent revisiting the bad parts.

Anyway, a week after the tree took the top off my house, the "Roof fairy" visited while I was here at the restaurant and replaced it. Good as new. I had a hunch these guys were behind it and refused to serve them sweet tea for a week.

Words were exchanged. They said not to kick a gift horse in the mouth. Not to bite the hand that feeds or some such nonsense.

Finally, Mrs. Daley left the farm to have a chat with me. She said it's rude to turn down generosity. For instance, back in the day, she looked the other way when we used the paved road out by her house as a drag strip. My pride ripped and roared about that. But I got her point and reinstated sweet tea rights.

The guys get to their feet. Without a word, Hank starts sweeping up. Dick takes out the trash, and Hank is in the back talking to Antoine.

"I'll have to ask Honey," he says in his deep voice.

Hank hollers, "Did you ever get the generator repaired?"

"It's on my to-do list," I holler back. My mile-long to-do list.

"Then you'll want to take anything perishable home."

I pop my head into the food delivery window. "You think the power is going to go out?"

"Good chance. I'm going to bring my spare generator over for the freezer. But if there's anything perishable in the fridge, I'd clear it out," Hank says.

"Antoine, you have the biggest family, you take what you can." I've ridden out countless storms, so I'm not nervous, except this will be a first with a baby if it comes to that.

I say, "The good thing is we won't get our big delivery until Monday, so we're fresh out of most things. But I'll take the sandwich cold cuts and cheese. You take the eggs."

I insist Buck, Dick, and Hank also take some food home, including the pies to their wives who I know will appreciate them—especially the apple which I only make seasonally.

By the time I pick Leonie up from Mara's, the wind howls something fierce and the bare branches wave and scratch the dark gray sky like fingernails. The thick clouds roll closer with nothing to stop them.

Just past sunset, a loud pop explodes outside on the street, instantly submerging us in darkness. Leonie startles and cries with fright.

I pace and sing until she settles, watching the scene outside as the fire crew shows up, the wind and rain lashing them. Lights flash. A large truck appears. Voices rise and fall.

Someone bangs on the screen door. Leonie cries again. I kiss her fuzzy little head and sing until she's quiet, wondering if this was what it was like for my mother, living in this very same trailer. What finally broke her? Or had she been that way all along?

Struggling against the wind to open the door, I find Jesse on the other side. Water drips from his broad sheriff's hat.

"Honey, you alright in there?"

"We're Hoggers. Of course we are," I say as the storm whips up a fierce tantrum outside.

"Sorry to bother you this late. A transformer blew and a live line is down out on the street. We're alerting all the residents to stay put or else risk electric shock."

"If that's the case, why aren't I looking at a BBQ deputy?"

"The area adjacent to your property and Shady Lane is clear. If residents want to leave, they'll have to walk through your yard. I don't advise that in this weather because of the way your property line comes up to those poles."

I think about the layout and nod, understanding what he means.

"The power company probably won't get out here until tomorrow, at least. You don't happen to have a generator?"

I shake my head. "Not here or at the restaurant." It's on the to-do list too.

Footsteps thud on the two rickety steps that lead to my front door. I imagine it's someone from the volunteer fire department.

Instead, Maddock fills the doorway, also dripping wet. "You're okay?"

"Why wouldn't I be?"

He shrugs sheepishly, maybe having forgotten that this isn't my first Gulf storm.

Jesse says, "I was going to offer to escort you to the restaurant if you wanted to weather things out over there. But if that generator is still—"

I interrupt, "Someone stole the copper off it."

His lips pinch with apology. "That was thirteen years ago."

"These things don't repair themselves, Jesse."

He pulls out a little notebook with a spiral on top and jots something down.

"If that's a Bail Honey Out Note, I don't want it."

"Don't be so stubborn," Jesse says.

Maddock's mouth lowers as if surprised by Jesse's audacity.

"Deputy Lawson, also make a note that you're the only person on the planet who can talk to me like that, and make sure to spread the word."

Jesse chortles. "It's because I'm practically your brother."

"From another mother."

"Have you been answering her letters?" he asks.

"How do you know she's been writing to me?"

"I saw her last month."

I huff. "If you know me so well, you should realize where not to stick your nose, Lawson."

"Isn't she adorable when she's mad?" Jesse asks Maddock.

As if he was just tagged to enter the fighting ring, Maddock looks up from my bookshelves, apparently noting my history book collection. "I definitely agree."

"Don't you dare start—" They've got me wound up. "Now, scram. You're both dripping water all over the place."

Jesse edges to the door as if knowing he's close to pushing me too far. "That's going to be the least of your problems come morning."

Maddock straightens to his full height. "You can come to the chateau with me."

I shake my head. "I couldn't impose."

"You and Leonie can and you will."

Jesse says, "That's a great idea. Pack up."

Hands on my hips, I say, "Excuse me, boys, I won't be told what to do."

"There's no power here. The pole is hung up in the tree that hangs over your roof—"

"It's a new roof."

"It's an old tree," Maddock counters.

"We're fine here."

"Not with a baby and not without power or water." Maddock's jaw is set.

"I have some extra jugs."

"Honey, this is Hurricane Hogan we're talking about."

"That's not its name."

Jesse intervenes, "Honest to goodness. I think it's a good idea to go over to the chateau. That place has stood this long."

"Are we really going to bring your judgment into this?"

"If you're talking about jumping off Picklecrick's Dam, that was fifteen years ago and a dare."

"It was during a lightning storm. Also, that just goes to show you, I can handle myself in a little weather."

"You were the one who jumped first," Jesse mutters.

I jut my chin. It can't be helped that I was a feral teenager. Leonie wiggles in my arms, bucking slightly as if she just now sees Maddock and wants him to hold her.

"I'd take her, but I'm all wet."

"What happened to your baby allergy?"

"I took an antihistamine."

I snort. "Well, I'm allergic to you."

"I have a whole box in the truck. Works like a charm." The corner of his lip jerks with a grin.

Jesse sputters with laughter. "Yep. Officer's orders. You three are definitely shacking up over at the chateau. Pack up, Honey. This building is officially condemned until further notice."

"You can't do that."

"Just did. Now, off with you before this place collapses on us."

"It's not going to—"

The creaking sound of dead wood about to give way comes from outside. My gut twists.

Maddock grabs a blanket from the sofa and arranges it so he

can take Leonie without getting her sopping wet. I hurry to the bedroom and pack a couple of bags, making sure to bring plenty of diapers. His shirt sits folded on top of my bureau and I consider taking it to return to him, but then I leave it ... and accidentally forget a pair of pajamas. He probably has another T-shirt I can borrow.

I go still in the doorway as my thoughts catch up with me. "Whoa, Honey. Easy does it."

Jesse gives me a look as he packs up all the identifiable baby stuff, including the rocking chair Thelma gave me.

Yup. Still thinking about Maddock and talking to myself. I think he's bad for my health. But I don't need an antihistamine. More like a Maddock inoculation.

Just before I head outside, I double back and grab the carton of eggs that I took from the restaurant earlier. I have a recipe I can make that's even better than crème brûlée.

Maddock has Leonie and her assortment of gear loaded into the truck, and I hop in the police SUV with Jesse. We follow right behind them with the rest of our stuff.

"She's so small, yet she requires so much stuff," he says.

Since he and Tallula are expecting, I say, "You'd better get prepared."

Overhead, the canopy of trees over the road that leads to the chateau whips and snaps in the blustery wind as rain splatters the windshield making for slow going.

I say, "Thanks for helping me out."

"The last time we were in a police cruiser together was after the drag race when Willy Spellman went in the ditch."

"Yeah, but we were in the backseat."

"That sounds—"

I interrupt, "It sounds bad no matter how far your mind is in the gutter."

"Thanks to Sawyer's community service, Hogwash's

gutters are clear, which means we shouldn't see much flooding. It's the wind that's the problem. Your house should be okay. This is just a precaution."

And I should proceed with caution because Jesse is wrong. It isn't only the wind that's the problem. Maddock makes me feel like I'm caught in a hurricane, blowing this way and that, hot and cold air clashing, sending me into the center where it's calm before thrusting me back into a storm of emotions.

"When you think about it, we both turned out okay," he says, oddly sentimental. "It's like God picked us up and turned us right around."

"You did take a tumble in a graveyard," I say.

"We call it an accident, but I think of it as an on-purpose because I found my purpose."

"Senior year, I think you were voted least likely to become a police officer."

He chuckles. "You mean most likely to go to jail. Who'd ever have thought you'd become a mother?"

"That was also an accident." I stop myself, belatedly realizing his meaning. "I mean, for my cousin. Probably. You remember her." Being Leonie's mom feels very purposeful. A blessing even though times like these are hard.

"Ah yes. The Queen of Hearts. She was worse than the two of us combined. Leonie got lucky with you."

"Yeah. An on-purpose."

"Funny, I noticed when we were at your place, her eyes are so much like Maddock's. What are the chances? You never know when some things are just meant to be."

I shake my head because she doesn't. Jesse is probably just playing matchmaker to take some of the pressure off of feeling obligated to look after me—Hogwash's single mom charity case. No one knows how Leonie came into my care. I've even let Molly speculate. If my cousin wanted anyone to know, she would've broadcast it. She has a big enough mouth. My mother has her to thank for winding up in jail. Neither one of them has any allegiance—not even to their own kin.

But Jesse is absolutely right. God must've had a hand in this. It's an on-purpose, and we both ended up with the better lot if you ask me.

I thank Deputy Lawson and am practically shoved inside the chateau—by the wind, not him. At the last moment, I catch the door behind me, keeping it from slamming and startling Leonie.

The scene in front of me takes my breath away.

There's Maddock, hair dripping wet, his hulking figure poised over Leonie who rests safely on a blanket on the table, legs and arms waving happily. He's like the Beast, only, his hand presses against his heart and liquid forms in his eyes.

# Chapter 10

## *The T-shirt*

U ntil now, I hadn't properly made eye contact with the baby. But when we got inside, she was fussing. I can't claim to have any idea how to change a diaper, but I figured I'd get things ready for when Honey got here.

Yeah, the dining room table isn't the ideal place, but I'll wipe it down later. Plus, Leonie's on top of a couple of blankets. The kid is powerful—especially those pipes. But I have enough sense to keep my eyes on her so she doesn't roll.

And that's just it. Her eyes are big and blue and somehow look past mine and—my heart does something weird. It's like my ribs crack open. My pulse is a mess. The second one is a result of Honey standing in the doorway, a bag in one hand along with a carton of eggs.

I have a strange sensation of déjà vu. Or future vu. I don't know what any of that means. But there's a strong sense of rightness inside that I've never before experienced.

It's like she's come home and this is our family.

But the look I'm getting is *Ew Beast* as if I'd lock her up here like in the old fairytale, which reminds me of when I teased her about kissing and she said that would be gross.

The woman is no-nonsense. But she's all beauty. Even half windblown from the rain after a long day. Her neck is long, forming smooth lines that disappear into her shoulders. I recall her wearing my T-shirt. She hasn't given it back. Maybe she burned it in effigy. Or perhaps she sleeps with it on her pillowcase.

I give my head a little shake because right now it's all over the place.

Pointing at Leonie, I say, "I think she needs a diaper change."

Honey bumps me out of the way with her hip and has Leonie clean, dry, and changed into a little sleep sack garment in under sixty seconds.

"You could be part of a pit crew."

"I was."

My brow bunches up. "I can't tell if you're joking."

"Where are you putting us?" Her gaze wanders to my chest, where moments before, I'd pressed my hand to my heart. The warmth and imprint remain similar to when I was a kid, and I'd do a belly flop into the lake, it would smart for hours afterward, only better.

My voice is scratchy even after I clear my throat. "I've been staying in the main suite on the second floor. You two stay up there. I'll—" He angles his head toward a leather couch that looks new.

It's Leonie's bedtime, and I set her Pack 'n Play next to the king-sized bed in the master bedroom. Honey stares at it.

To put her mind at ease, I say, "As I said, I'm taking the couch."

"I can't sleep in here."

"I understand you're a headstrong woman, but I assure you—"

"Why does everyone say that about me?"

"I wasn't done. You're also incredibly stubborn."

"So I've heard."

"It's adorable."

"Maddock ..." Her tone is one of warning.

"It's good to be strong. And it's obvious you have a head on your shoulders." I smooth a damp piece of hair behind her ear. "But you could try to be less stubborn."

"You mean please try to be more adorable?"

"I mean someone stubborn burned me once."

"But you're a firefighter. Don't you know how to put out fires?"

"Safety first."

Honey blinks a few times as if my comments catch up with her and she doesn't have the energy left to fight yet battles with herself about how much she wants to collapse onto the bed—it's plush. "I'm still in the twin I've been sleeping in since I was a kid."

"Then you'll sleep like a baby with all that room." I gesture to the king.

She barks a laugh and then claps her hand over her mouth before whispering, "That saying is a lie! All lies! Babies are the worst sleepers on the planet. The saying should be *I'm going to sleep like a lumberjack who's been chopping wood all day.* That would knock someone out cold."

"Or a firefighter that's on the last leg of his shift ..."

She nods and taps the air. "Precisely."

Or a firefighter on paid leave who has to repeatedly fight a blaze in his mind, in his heart, in his hands. I shove them in my pockets because right now I have the urge to slide my arm around Honey's shoulders as we watch the baby peacefully slumber.

My breath shakes when I exhale. "Well, I'll say goodnight. If you need anything, let me know."

"Actually, in my hurry, I, um, didn't, um, pajamas—"

She doesn't finish before the words are out of my mouth. "Do you want another T-shirt?"

Honey bites her lip and nods. "Yeah, that would be great. I'll get your other one back to you, too."

I wave my hand dismissively. "Not to worry. I have loads."

Her gaze flickers. Something crackles between us and it's not from the lightning or thunder outside.

I'd like to say I sleep soundly, but the wind whips against the old windowpanes, and my thoughts whirl in a torrent of blue eyes and the way Leonie seems to fill up a part of my heart I didn't realize was empty. How Honey could very well hold that same heart in her hands if I let her. And what the future might look like—I didn't think I'd still be in Hogwash no less considering staying here.

The next morning, gray light pierces my eyelids and a babbling sound along with a soft clacking comes from the kitchen.

I sniff the air as the storm last night comes back. I'd heard the crack of the transformer above the wind and instinct had me rushing out to the main road. The Hogwash volunteer fire department was already on the scene and evaluating the situation. Having dealt with countless instances of the very same thing out west, I jumped into the zone—well, not literally with the downed wires—and took charge.

I hope that Honey's house held up. She's as strong as she is sweet—the woman, not the single wide. But she's also proud. That house means a lot to her, and I imagine it would be a big blow, and not just financially, if there's damage.

After a yawn and a stretch, I get up and wander to the kitchen. "Good morning."

Honey, with Leonie on her hip, turns from the stovetop. "Morning. You didn't have ingredients for pancakes, otherwise I would've made them on account of your hospitality."

"You seem refreshed."

She fights a grin. "Leonie slept through the night, which means I did too. The first on record."

"Yesterday must've tuckered you both out."

"Yeah. Also, that bed is super comfortable."

"Half the week I spend at the firehouse, sleeping on a bunk so my reasoning was to invest in a good mattress. I special ordered the same one I have back home."

"The chateau hasn't looked this good in well over a decade."

I pick up on this and add it to a reference she made a while ago. "Did you used to spend time here?"

"Unfortunately."

"Is that why you didn't want to stay?"

She shifts from foot to foot, then sets Leonie in her little vibrating seat with the light-up toys. "Not exactly."

Leonie fusses so I pick her up and she settles right down, babbling again.

Honey huffs like she's annoyed that I have the magic touch. "So what are you making instead of flapjacks?"

"*Bouillie au lait.*"

"More boo? I assure you the chateau isn't haunted." Except maybe by the ghosts of the past, I understand that all too well … or maybe the ghosts of what'll never be.

It's absurd, but every time I look at Leonie's eyes, like right now, it's like my own are staring back at me.

She pronounces the mixture on the stove *boo yoh lay* and explains it's similar to custard. Honey flits around like this is her kitchen. If I squint, I can imagine us—a happy family with the wooden screen door flapping open and shut as kids run in and out.

I jolt. Leonie grabs my thumb, squeezes, and juts her legs out before one of her socks flies off. Honey picks it up and stuffs it over my thumb.

I meet her gaze and we both laugh.

"Whoops. Sorry. That was Mom Brain. I must not have slept as well as I thought."

"After we eat, I'll go check on the power lines. Do you have the electric company's app? They should be able to tell you when to expect power to be restored."

Honey sets two bowls on the table. "I have a flip phone, so no."

"Is that by choice? Are you a Luddite?"

We talk about people who eschew modern technology for the most part. I learn that her older model device isn't by choice. And yet, she has a Porsche and used to spend time here at the chateau.

I steal a glance at her eyes as she dips into the custard boo stuff. There are secrets there, that's for sure.

After a second cup of coffee and a shower, I drive to Honey's house and return with bad news ... the kind I don't want to deliver when she meets me with a bright smile as if happy to see me.

"You've made some real progress here," she whispers. Leonie must be down for her morning nap.

"I have a lot more to go, which brings me to the question I've been wanting to ask."

"I have a question for you, too. When I was making breakfast, I found an old cookbook." She strides toward the kitchen to show me.

The frayed red linen hardcover features the words *Cookbook* with a basket of apples in the center. Inside, three gold rings bind the brittle pages.

Honey asks, "Do you mind if I borrow it?"

"You can have it ... but this brings me to my question. You can have it only if you live here."

She blinks a few times as if not believing her ears, as if I'd finally conceded and called a flapjack a pancake.

Then I say, "Because I have bad news."

Her face crumbles as if she knows the tree went through the roof.

And I want nothing more than to be this woman's shelter in the storm.

# Chapter 11

## *A Mental Health Day*

Do I regret spending the day upstairs in the master bedroom pouting like a princess who didn't get her way? Only slightly.

I wonder how many blows I can take. This one is massive. Turns out my roof can only take one per season. The weight of the telephone pole and the tree couldn't support it and everything crashed into my house as the rain and wind pummeled it overnight.

But that's not the worst of it. Maddock Witt thinks he can just waltz into this town and take over. Well, technically, he can since he owns it. But he has no claim to my heart ... or my lips. It's not like I think about kissing him. Much.

It makes me feel all twitchy inside like a lovesick teenager. I tug the pillow over my chest and hug it. Where did that notion even come from?

The flaming windstorm between us has to stop. Things need to go back to exactly how they were before he nearly crashed into my Porsche, and that's final.

Tomorrow, I have to return to reality ... However, right now,

Leonie's tootsies are looking particularly adorable and perfect for a game of Piggy, so can you blame me for snuggling with my baby and generally wallowing while the beast of a man downstairs repeatedly comes to my aid?

Thankfully, the restaurant is okay. But I'm not. The emotional weight of my memories in this chateau press against me. I refuse to revisit that time in my life.

I won't resort to crime like my mother and cousin. For them, it was a game, a lifestyle.

Before Leonie came along, saving, scrimping, and basically limping through life on fumes was acceptable. A necessity at times. But she needs diapers, and no one needs a pumpkin spice latte no matter what they tell you. Okay, fine. The Coffee Loft has been advertising and there have been moments when I've considered offering a kidney in exchange, but what if Leonie someday needs it? I'm a mom now and my responsibilities are real. So are diapers—even the cloth ones we use because I've worked out a trade with Debbie's Diaper Care to cater her annual customer appreciation party in exchange for a discount.

Affording this kid, no less figuring out her care so I can work to earn money to afford her needs, is like a mental and physical gymnastics loop, treadmill, and hamster wheel all at once.

So yeah, I've taken my first mental health day EVER.

Yes, even after I lost Cory, I didn't let a day go by that I didn't persevere. Well, I did take up smoking, but that habit was short-lived. Lollipops to the rescue. I could really go for one right now. When my mother's debt collectors called, I carried on. And when this baby arrived in my life, I forged ahead.

But now I've stopped and I'm scared I won't ever be able to get up.

Leonie blows a raspberry as if in response. As if to call *Hogwash.*

Unlike my car, I've never run out of gas, but my tank feels so close to empty—something wet drips onto the pillowcase. Remembering where I am, I wipe away the tears, draw my baby toward me, and close my eyes.

Later, when I wake up, the sky is dim as dusky gray-violet light settles in the bayou. The storm and everything that transpired hurtles toward me, but not before I remember a dream.

I was on the long, lonely road between Hogwash and Poupeville. I carried an empty gas can. A man approached, took it out of my hand, and rested his on my shoulder. With a wink, he went on his way.

Only, his eyes were Leonie's eyes ... and I realize she's not in the bed with me. I bolt upright.

A cold sweat breaks out across my forehead and neck. They say babies can roll and fall off beds and surfaces easily. Of course, there's the wall on one side, I built a pillow fort, and made a barrier with my body, but she's not here.

I rush downstairs, but before I reach the kitchen, a low voice sings, "You are my Sunshine." Leonie lets out a happy little roar and a laugh. I go still and lean against the wall in the dark dining room, catching my breath. An upwelling of emotion threatens me again and I wipe away tears—they're a mixture of happy and sad tears. Happy because Maddock unexpectedly appeared in my life. Sad because he's only here temporarily.

Sending up a prayer, I ask for help.

And wouldn't you know it, the next song Maddock sings is an old Beatles tune about getting the help of friends?

Could I call him that? I think about who I'd consider a friend and frown. I know a lot of people—have a patchwork of helpers, but are they friends? Do I let people get close to me? Am I a friend to them? The answer isn't a resounding yes and that feels like a problem.

The screen door opens and closes, wafting the scent of grilled burgers into the house. I peer around the corner to find the kitchen in use and Leonie's various play containers where I left them. She's not here, but relief washes through me because he must've taken her outside rather than leave her unattended. But the grill! It's hot and I've heard stories about propane tanks spontaneously combusting.

Being a new mom brought with it an inordinate amount of new dangers. Things I once thought were innocuous are now potential threats ... and they're everywhere. And this is coming from me, someone who lived fast and furious for a long time.

Through the window, Maddock and Leonie gaze off the back porch, far from the grill, and it looks like he's pointing to a peacock wandering across the back lawn.

Letting out a breath, I turn around to go back upstairs because I should've brushed my hair and teeth, but Maddock and Leonie come back inside.

Turning around and entering the kitchen as if I'd casually just walked downstairs, I say, "There you are—" I'm about to scold Maddock and warn him never to take a cub from a sleeping mama bear again, but why would I think there would be an *again?*

Also, seeing him holding the little bean pod baby outward so she can see what he sees—me—makes my heart hiccup.

"There's our Sleeping Beauty." Maddock's gaze skims me from head to toe and a smile forms on his lips.

Feeling self-conscious, I smooth my hair and wheeze a nervous laugh. "I'm not pageant-ready by a long shot."

"I'd love to hear more about that time in your life." His grin is flirty and his eyes wander over me as if he likes what he sees. I question his taste because right now, I rate high on the swamp witch scale.

I greet Leonie and she waves her arms happily. Glancing

up at Maddock, I answer his question. "My mother and cousin pressured me into joining so they could rob the judges and other entrants while we were on stage. I was always the distraction."

If the truth shocks him or he thinks I'm joking, he doesn't show it. Instead, his eyes dance and sparkle. "You certainly are." Giving his head a shake, he adds, "Dinner is almost done. Made burgers, coleslaw, and—"

"You made coleslaw?"

He tips his head to the side. "Why the sound of surprise?"

There's also grilled corn on the cob and watermelon on the counter.

"I didn't figure you for a cook."

"I'm a firefighter."

"Exactly."

"At least once a week, I'm on chef duty for the guys."

"Burgers. It fits."

"And I make a mean fettuccini Alfredo, get seconds requests for my chicken soup, and there are never leftovers when I make pulled pork nachos. Still working on my rib game, though. Dish up."

I reach for Leoni and he arches an eyebrow, stopping me in my tracks.

Maddock repeats, "Fill up a plate and then you can take the baby."

"Fine. Sheesh. No reason to be mean about it." But the idea of eating a meal off a plate, no less sitting down and one that he prepared for me after not doing so in nearly five months sounds like a gift—one I'm not going to turn down, thanks to Mrs. Daley's lecture.

As if an afterthought, Maddock says, "I wasn't being mean. More like direct. Has anyone ever told you that you're stubborn?"

"You've mentioned. But other than you and Jesse, no."

He grunts. "Probably because they know how you'll respond."

I'm about to do just that when Leonie laughs.

Point taken.

Nothing like becoming a parent to learn humility. Unless you're my mother.

As I take a seat and Maddock sets a burger on my bun, I think back to all the nights we spent in this very house—her laughter filtering from the other room as she entertained gullible gamblers. Meanwhile, my stomach rumbled with hunger—for food and a way out of that life.

I jump to my feet. "Wait. What about Leonie?"

He gestures I calm down, or sit down, I'm not sure. I'm about ready to karate chop his big hand, not that I know how without breaking my own. "She ate an hour ago."

I gasp, glancing at the food on our plates. "What did you feed her?"

"Milk."

"She's too young. She can't have regular—"

"Chill. I gave her the baby milk you'd put in the fridge."

"How much? What was the temperature? Did you clean—?"

Maddock looks me square in the face. "Honey, I understand that you're a do-it-yourselfer. But I work as part of a team. I called the Coffee Loft and Tallula gave me Mara's number. She walked me through what to do."

I slouch into my chair, relieved. "Thank you."

The corner of his lip lifts in a smile. "No need to thank me."

Leonie, now seated in the play saucer, kicks her feet, but for once, her sock doesn't fly off.

I pick up my hamburger to take a bite, then set it down. A

nagging question holds my appetite hostage. "Before, you had a very clear aversion to babies ... and me. What changed?"

I notice he's hardly touched his meal as he makes sure we have everything we need. He stops and looks at me again as if maybe I have the answer. "I don't know."

It's not like Maddock and I cleared the air—it's as gummy and humid as ever, at least outside—but it does seem like we turned a page.

While we eat, we talk about the damage in town from the storm. We also discuss Leonie and randomly our opinions on tattoos—we both have one. His is from when he graduated from the fire academy. I won't tell him what or where mine is—a pair of checkered racing flags on my hip. For once, we're like two normal people. Like friends. And not like a pair of wolves at each other's throats. Funny, what breaking bread can do.

We take turns cleaning up and then take an after-dinner walk, which also feels very normal. I wear Leonie in the strappy pouch thing Maddock helped me figure out how to assemble. I've had it for months but didn't know which clips to connect where and every time I tried to use it, she and I both ended up in a tangle.

The night is cool, the stars barely visible above, but the landscaping lights illuminate a path through what was once a beautiful garden and is now cut back like a toddler was set loose with a tractor.

"JQ suggested I consult Backyard Dreamscapes to figure out what to do out here. They did a nice job on what he calls his oasis. But that'll come later. For now, I just wanted to clear out the old growth to make way for the new."

A lump grows in my throat. "You've been hanging out with JQ?"

"And Jesse."

A train of thought threatens to run away with emotions I

thought were old and that I'd cleared out. JQ was Cory's best friend. He and Jesse were enemies. But now Maddock dares to somehow bring them all together.

I harrumph. "Why would you hang out with them?"

Not surprisingly, he shoots me a look like I'm the one who kicked over the statue in the corner of the garden and ran away with its head—that was Jesse and it was a long time ago. We needed an additional bowling ball for a game we were playing on the drag strip out past Daley's farm.

Maddock answers, "Because they're nice guys. Remind me of Leyton and some of the others on the crew back home."

"When are you leaving? Going back home?"

"Not sure yet."

I have the sudden need to escape that answer. "We should go back to the house. Leonie needs a bath."

I could spend the time in the bathroom with my baby reflecting on my behavior and comments. Instead, I stew in how unfair everything is. I didn't ask for a tree to go through my roof or the power outage to render my side of the street to be dark until further notice. Meanwhile, the Coffee Loft and every other business on the north side of Main carries on while, I, the one who didn't even ask to run a restaurant, am struggling to stay afloat.

Arson is but one of the crimes that sent Mama to the clink. In an ill-advised game of cards bender, she won and then subsequently lost the Laughing Gator Grille back to the original owner. Thinking the insurance transfer had gone through, she set the place ablaze. Thankfully, our volunteer firefighting crew extinguished it before more than the rear entry and kitchen were damaged. I used my racing winnings to pay George and Lucille Guidry, the owners, off instead of entering Nationals. But then they walked away, leaving me with the mess to deal with while Mama went to jail anyway on several other charges to boot—namely grand larceny.

The cheers and jeers at my pity party go quiet when I gaze into Leonie's eyes. At least I have this sweet baby covered in bubbles, who is happy, healthy, and really truly my sunshine. I sing her the song that Maddock had earlier.

With a smile, she splashes me and lets out a happy roar. Her eyes sparkle. They're the exact shade of Maddock's with the dark blue center and the lighter ring like the teardrops on a peacock's feather.

After wrapping her up like a little dumpling, I go into the bedroom to put her in fresh clothes, when I find Maddock plugging something into the wall.

"Excuse me."

He shields his eyes. "Sorry. I was just hooking up the baby monitor."

"We're both clothed, er, covered. I meant what are you doing in here?" I'm wearing his T-shirt, but that's so I didn't get my outfit soaked. There's no telling when I'll be able to do laundry again. "Where did you get a baby monitor?"

"Lexi. She said to give it a test spin."

I glance at the package. "It's the Baby Watch Pro. Thelma and Betsy got it for her baby shower."

"Well, it works." He wiggles the handheld portion and starts to exit, then over his shoulder, says, "See you downstairs in a few."

I refuse to be told what to do—sit like a dog at dinner or come when ordered. Or even heel. I'm not someone's puppet. Then again, I did say I come with strings.

Once again, tears spill from my eyes. They're silent ones— the kind that I hardly let myself spare when I found out Cory was dead. On nights when I wasn't sure how I was going to keep the electricity running that week. When my dreams of going to Nationals were dashed.

I'm convinced this house is haunted—definitely by ghosts of my past. I'll make arrangements to stay somewhere else. Anywhere else.

But that doesn't happen. The rest of the week passes and the restaurant remains closed. Workers are stretched thin—along with the tarp over my roof—and the insurance lapsed. I don't expect Hank, Dick, and Buck are going to replace it this time.

But Maddock lets us stay at the chateau, feeds us, and clothes us. Well, me. I now have four of his T-shirts.

It's Friday night and the floor outside the bedroom door creeks. It's open a crack and a shadow falls across it. Leonie just fell asleep and I tip-toe-run across the wooden floor, desperate for him not to wake her.

She had a gassy spell this afternoon and was generally fussy. I also think she's getting a tooth. The internet says she's on the younger side, but I have a feeling.

Finger to my lips in the universal *Shh* motion, I mouth, *She just fell asleep.*

He gestures me into the hallway.

Seriously, this guy. Who does he think he is?

I hesitate.

He tips his head toward the stairs.

My lips bunch up.

Chest rising, he inhales and then mouths, *Please.*

I can't say no to that, but I won't do it in one of his T-shirts. When I'm wearing them, his lips curl into a half smile and his eyes are blue flame. Plus, it's huge on me, so I feel like a child. A grown-up woman child with a baby.

My mother's words, *Don't be such a baby* when I'd show reluctance to follow her orders to fool people into falling for her traps filter back. I bristle but another part of me wants to take younger me by the hand and promise her everything will work out. But is that true?

Safe and snug in the Pack 'n Play, I resolve that Leonie's childhood will be nothing like mine.

Baby monitor in hand, I meet Maddock at the foot of the stairs. His mouth is a flirty, cocky grin like he knew I'd give in. My stomach tightens because I want to resist this man.

The best I can do is sling my arms across my chest and in my sassiest tone, ask, "Well?"

"I'm leaving." He walks down the hall, and then casually over his shoulder, he says, "First, I want to show you something."

Even though curiosity tugs me toward him, I dig in my heels and don't budge.

# Chapter 12

## *Beauty & the Beast*

I'm nearly through the door to the chateau's library when I realize Honey didn't follow me. She remains at the foot of the stairs, her expression a mess of puzzle pieces that don't fit together—sadness flickers in her eyes, her nostrils flare with anger, and resolve keeps her lips in a thin line.

Her full, pretty, pink sassy lips.

"Are you coming?" I ask.

Jaw set, she says, "I should pack."

"Honey, take your foot off the gas."

"What's that supposed to mean?" she snaps.

"Come in here and I'll tell you."

With one hand on the banister, she seems to argue with herself. It's not that I want to boss her around. No, she does plenty well managing herself like a C-suite executive. I've learned that if I'm subtle, I won't get her attention. She'll speed away before I have a chance to remind her that not every piece of news is bad news.

"This isn't the scene of a crime," I say, eager to show her something I think she'll like.

She practically cackles.

"Please come here," I repeat.

Arms across her chest, she stomps over.

"You were a real delight as a teenager, weren't you?"

"Ha ha," she says dryly.

With Honey, I soften, want to smooth her rough edges and show her that not everything needs to be a battle for the survival of the fittest. It's another thing I cannot explain when it comes to this woman.

"What?" she snaps.

I was staring, gazing at her. Her eyes are beautiful, but they're not her daughter's. Honey might come across as tough as nails on the outside, but beneath all the armor is pure sugar ... and I'd be a crazy liar if I said I didn't want a taste.

I sweep the library door open and flick on the light.

The room stands empty with two large windows opposite the door.

"Before you say anything snide or smart—" I tap on my phone and show her digital renderings of the library I commissioned and plan to have built.

She tilts her head and then squints. "Is that a rolling ladder on the bookshelf?"

"Sure is."

Honey Hamilton is a limited edition, a one-of-a-kind and I want her to have something all her own. After seeing the books on her shelves ruined from the storm, I had the idea to make this a place for her to escape ... and yes, that means her living here for as long as she wants—even though I'm heading back west soon.

She peeks at the design again. "Those chairs look comfortable."

"Great for sitting and reading."

She snorts a laugh. "Lucky you."

The words I want to say stick on my tongue. I'd originally intended to use this town as a revenge plot. Emberly wanted to distance herself from this little backwater bayou. Getting the country club elites whispering about her connection to a place like this would take her down a few pegs. But Hogwash is an underdog and I want to see it succeed. With that came the urge to make the chateau Honey and Leonie's home.

She rejects pity, but also generosity. Edging toward the door, she turns off the light, submerging us in darkness. Deprived of my sense of sight, less than an arm's length away, she radiates warmth. Her honeysuckle scent fills my nose. My pulse gets messy and my thoughts turn foggy—not a single one is clear.

Time to walk it off. Breathe. Get my head on straight.

I sit down in the living room and sling my arm across the back of the couch, which has also doubled as my bed, but I fold up my sheets every morning.

Honey remains standing. "You said you're leaving."

"Duty calls. I have a short-term assignment back in Nevada. But I'll supervise the renovations from there. Meanwhile, you're welcome to stay."

I don't know what the future of my career looks like, but I'd be an idiot to turn down Leyton's offer.

She cocks her hip and plants her hand on it. "If—?"

"If what?" I ask.

"There's a catch. You want me to do something in exchange."

I tip my head from side to side. "Well, not exactly, though it would be great if you were my eyes on the ground. Not in a hands-on capacity. But since you're familiar with the space—" I was going say she could oversee the workers, make sure they're not slacking off on renovations but she interrupts.

"You have no idea."

I pat the spot next to me. "Tell me."

"It's a long story."

"My flight doesn't leave until tomorrow."

As if I twisted her arm instead of inviting her to join me on the leather piece of furniture, she stalks over and plops down, feet planted on the floor, elbows folded across her knees.

Silence threads between us.

"Go on," I coax.

"It's not that long a story. Actually."

"You don't have to tell me. But you can tell me about yourself."

"Pfft. Yeah. Okay. I'm sure you want to hear that."

"I do."

She peers at me over her shoulder. "I'm Honey Hamilton. Brown eyes. Five nine. I don't know how much I weigh. Probably not enough. Ironically, I run the Laughing Gator Grille. Yes, I have a police record. But I was only guilty a few of the times."

I smile. "Is that so? But you're so sweet."

"We both know that's not true."

I click my tongue in disagreement. "You left out a few things. You're a history buff."

She slackens as if touched that I noticed. "True. I won the Miss Louisiana Pageant because I recited Lincoln's Gettysburg Address."

"Ironic. Let's hear it."

She stuffs down a smile. "What?"

"Recite it to me."

She shakes her head. "I—"

"I don't know those historical words by heart, but Lincoln didn't start it with *I*." I lean closer.

To my surprise, she doesn't shift away.

"That's just it, Honey Hamilton. Brown eyes. Five nine.

Just right weight—though I'll make you dinner anytime. Owner of the Laughing Gator Grille. I've only known you for a month, but so far, nothing you do starts with *I*. You're a *you* person. You help others."

Something ripples across her features as she takes a deep breath, then begins the famous speech by President Lincoln.

We're both quiet when she concludes. She faltered once or twice but got right on track. I can't help but believe those words also guided her life—what may have been a tough one. A life she's tried to drive away from but can't seem to get past the town limits without being pulled back.

"That was amazing. Profound."

"You can thank Abe."

I chuckle. "What else don't I know about you?"

"Everything." Her eyes sparkle.

I instantly regret agreeing to the job offer from Leyton. I want to sit on this couch until I know everything there is to know about this woman. But she'd never tell me. I have to witness it. Live it. Despite being able to recite all two hundred and sixty-eight words of that address, Honey is an action person, which I suppose is at the heart of what Lincoln intended.

I open the coffee table and take out a deck of cards. "Found packs of these all over the house. Looks like Tickle liked to play a round. When on overnights at the firehouse, we'll sometimes play poker."

"Tickle was a gambler. Poker was his main game. A real *brigand*." With her accent, it sounds like Honey says *brie gone*.

"What does that mean?"

"He was a bandit, wily."

I glance around the room, imagining the man who left riddles on his tombstone filling this space. "How do you know?"

"This is Hogwash Holler. Telling stories is what we do."

"It's a shame his descendants didn't keep up with this place. I'll change that."

"But you're not a Tickle."

"Does that matter?"

Her shoulder lifts like the residents of this town had been waiting for someone with that last name to swoop in and save it. "I suppose not."

"Do you play cards?" I shuffle them between my hands.

She scoffs like I just asked if she lives and breathes. "Yeah, of course."

"I had to teach Leyton—who later became Captain at my fire station—how to play War. So not everyone comes equipped with card playing skills."

"We call that one *Bataille*." She pronounces it *bah tie*, which suddenly makes me hungry for Pad Thai.

"I'll be right back."

I go to the kitchen and return with a bowl of peanuts and two bottles of root beer from the Penny Gamble. I'm not trying to trick Honey into telling me anything or wager her Porsche in a game. No, I just want to spend time with her.

I shuffle the cards properly and then deal them before giving her half the peanuts.

She chuckles. "Are we betting with these?"

"I'm short on change." But glad I didn't have that quarter on my first day here.

We play three card poker and then she teaches me *bourrè* which is similar to spades. Eventually, we graduate to baccarat. As the peanut piles grow and diminish, each of us winning and losing at different points, I learn that Hogan Tickle had a daughter who had a son who then had a son. I'm about to up the ante and go still, my handful of peanuts hovering.

"Are you sure about that genealogy?"

She gives one sharp nod. "Didn't you see the family tree on the gathering room wall?"

I shake my head.

Honey wears a wicked grin. "After I win, I'll show you."

"Oh, you're not winning," I counter, putting on my game face.

But she smokes me.

After a suitable amount of gloating, Honey says, "Do you still want to see the family tree? Could be something you want to preserve during the restoration."

"I'm surprised I didn't notice it."

Honey leads me to what she calls the gathering hall.

She tugs aside the tapestry on the wall. Underneath, the plaster is chipped, but the edge of a painting featuring foliage comes into view. I go into the hall, grab a stool, and pull the tapestry down.

Honey gasps. "That *canaille*." This one she pronounces *cah nie*.

"Cat night?"

"No, that sneak. She—" Lips tight, Honey points.

I lower from the stool and see someone spray-painted a bunch of red blobs that kind of look like bloated, broken, and drippy heart shapes on the wall.

I scratch my head, recalling the deputy's comment the first time we were here. "Do you mean *he*? Did Jesse do that?"

"No, it was my cousin. She fancied herself the Queen of Hearts. My mother always reminded her that she was merely a princess. Mama wore the crown in our crime family."

"You come from a criminal family?" I clear my throat, wishing I'd sounded more measured.

She looks me straight in the eyes. "Of course I do."

I'm not sure how, *of course*, fits into that statement or her background, but I cannot help but watch as she traces her fingers over the paint.

"You can still see a bit here and over here. Hogan is at the top with his wife, Eloise, not to be confused with Penny. She came first. After Eloise died, well, I guess it was a bridge they couldn't cross. Hogan and Eloise did have a daughter, though." She points to the spot where her name would've been. "Mireille married a steamship captain who later came to own a fleet. I imagine Tickle was pleased about that. They had a son shortly before Tickle passed away. His dying wish was for the Tickle name to carry on."

"Was his wish granted?"

"Their son, Blair, had a hyphen, which wasn't common in 1959, but yeah. Blair got married and divorced but died shortly thereafter."

"Did they keep the hyphen?"

"No, which is probably why this property somehow ended up in your hands rather than remaining in the Tickle family."

That means my ex must've originally been a Tickle, even though her last name was Jacobi. I peer at the faint family tree, wondering if I'll see her information. It's not here unless it's under the spray paint. My thoughts snag on what Honey said about Hogan's line going daughter, son, son—my ex would've come along after the second son, but that doesn't make sense. Then again, Tickle didn't leave his fortune to his direct descendants, so who knows how the estate shook out in probate.

I'm far more interested in Honey's history. "So, how do you fit into all this?"

"What do you mean?"

"You seem to know a lot."

"No more than anyone else in Hogwash." But Honey's neck stiffens, and I can't help but wonder what cards she keeps close to her vest.

# Chapter 13

## *Fireman Carry*

**M**addock has given me a lot to think about and even more I don't want to think about—namely, the past. But in a weird time loop, my mind sticks on how he's leaving for at least six weeks, which makes me think that all this will soon just be a memory.

The man blew into my life like a wrecking ball on fire, and I'm not sure I want to stop the destruction because that means maybe we can build something new—a future. But I have strings—adorable ones. Leonie and I come as a pair.

Mama sent yet another letter asking me about Ambrette's baby. Says she has information and insists I call or write at the very least. I won't be giving her the time of day now or anytime soon.

I'd rather put my hand in a blender than listen to her lies.

Thankfully, the restaurant is now open, keeping me from spending more time in my head. However, I'm now housing a family of rodents despite the big blue tarp over the hole in the roof of my trailer. If only Minou would do her job. Instead, she's made herself at home, living the high life at the chateau.

I'd like to pick myself up by my bootstraps, get up on the single-wide's roof, and fix the thing myself. But I know nothing about framing or shingles and I already received one courtesy roof from the kind people in my community. I don't think they have another spare lying around.

If it weren't for Maddock, I'd be in a dire, desperate situation.

It makes me feel small, helpless, and foolish.

I need a lollipop.

Mid-morning, Molly sidles up to the counter with a gleam in her eyes that tells me she knows something she shouldn't or is about to ask a question that's none of her business.

I get both.

"I've noticed some suspicious activity. I think someone has been prowling around the Tickle property at night."

"It's probably the crocogator."

"You might want to take precautions or let me investigate." Then, without a segue, she spends the next ten minutes asking me about Maddock's grooming, eating, and sleeping habits.

I see her angle. She has the hots for the firefighter and wants to know everything about him. This makes sweat prickle my hairline. "Is this an interrogation?"

Her eyebrows lift with a smile. "I prefer to think of it as an interview."

"In that case, no comment."

She inclines her head and leans close. "But you've been spending a lot of time together."

"In separate sections of the house."

She adds, "He buys you beignet buns."

"He also got biscuits for Frodo."

Molly jots something down, then says, "But I see the way you look at him."

The corner of my lip twitches. She's not entirely wrong about that.

Late in the afternoon, after picking Leonie up from Lexi's house, I return to the chateau to find Maddock loading the bed of his truck with boxes.

I haven't quite accepted that he's going to let us live here. Nor do I like the way the idea of him leaving makes me feel.

Least of all, I'm not a fan of how it's making me feel: like a raccoon that found the snack drawer, gobbled up its contents, and has been hopped up on espresso beans all day.

Oh wait, that's me.

Maddock stops at the foot of the stairs that lead to the kitchen as I mount them, Leonie in my arms. She waves hers, eager for him to hold her. He sets down the box and the two exchange a sickeningly adorable greeting. She pats his cheeks, and he nuzzles her, eliciting a peel of laughter. Then she kind of bites his nose and he laughs. It probably tickles. Raspberries blown on her belly come next, which results in a fit of giggles. They both make nonsensical happy noises.

While they're occupied, I peek in the box Maddock set on the ground. It contains a Corning Ware bowl, a few Pyrex baking dishes, a citrus juicer, and some other stuff—mostly kitchen items neither my mother nor scavengers thought were valuable. But they're vintage and well-made.

"What are you doing with all this?"

Without interrupting his motorboat lips while Leonie claps his ears and laughs with glee, Maddock says, "Clearing out odds and ends. Figured I could donate it on my way out of town tomorrow."

"No! You can't get rid of this." I pick up the box.

"It's junk."

"No, it's treasure."

"I thought you didn't believe in that."

"I don't. It's just that this is part of history. If you intend to restore the Tickle Chateau, it has to contain original items."

"It's not going to be a museum. We're going to live here."

I stagger backward. "We?"

He looks slightly sheepish. "I mean, yeah. For now. If you want."

I've gotten the sense that Maddock wants to help me out like I'm some pity-charity-single mom case. But I've gotten this far on my own. I can do it without being a tax write-off.

He adds, "No pressure."

But that's just what I've felt. So much pressure from every direction: the past with my mother, the present with the restaurant and taking care of Leonie, and the looming future with wanting to do everything I can so her life doesn't turn out like mine.

My thoughts turn foggy and I get dizzy. My knees suddenly feel like they're going to buckle. I reach for the handrail but miss as my vision blurs. A steady hand lands on mine as my thoughts fade and my surroundings turn spotty.

"Honey. It's okay. I've got you." Like an octopus, Maddock somehow manages to take the box from my hands while holding onto Leonie and me.

I struggle to return to full consciousness, knowing I need to take care of her.

"Honey, let me help you. Leonie is safe. She's just upset I stopped blowing raspberries on her belly. We need to get you inside."

Then I'm upside down, knocking me half back into reality.

Maddock swept me off my feet and now holds me in a fireman carry. My long hair splays toward the ground as he marches up the steps and into the kitchen. Not going to lie, I have a good view of his backside. He works out. Probably hits leg day hard. Also, I can feel the ripple of his firm muscles under his T-shirt.

So I don't let myself get too carried away, I protest, "What are you doing? Put me down."

Leonie sits in her bouncer and goes quiet as if trying to puzzle out what's happening. From my unusual position, I wave at her and play peek-a-boo around Maddock's side. She giggles.

He says, "I'll put you down if you promise me you'll eat something."

I start to protest, but my stomach growls. All I had today were two glasses of sweet tea. I can thank myself for the free refill, but not for skipping two meals.

An upside-down pastry box sits on the counter. Scratch that. I'm the one who is still upside down. With his arm still wrapped around my legs, Maddock flips open the lid with his free hand and passes me a muffin.

"What are you doing?" I'm not sure where to put my arms and fight the urge to wrap them around him. I bet his stomach is tightly etched with abs of steel.

Mine is empty.

He waves the muffin by my face. "It's a cinnamon apple streusel muffin."

My nose twitches at the delicious scent, but I sling my arms in front of my chest. "Ew. Gross."

"Ew. Gross. Like kissing. Is that what you think?"

"Absolutely?" I lie.

"Applelutely?"

My smile cracks.

He asks, "How about a beignet bun?"

"Bag nut?" I almost laugh despite myself. "It's pronounced *ben yay.*"

"Okay, Pancake Queen. How about I make you some flapjacks?"

"Pancakes and flapjacks aren't the same as mispronouncing beignet. Those are two different foods. I'm merely correcting your phonetics."

He takes a sugar cookie with icing and little autumn leaf sprinkles out of the box. "Can I tempt you with this?"

He's tempting with his thick hair that begs for me to run my hands into it. His stubble-covered cheeks. Full lips ... Even though I can't see that side of him from this position, his image is permanently painted in my head.

I seal my mouth and shake my head from side to side.

As if more fatigued by my stubborn refusal to do what he says, than by holding me over his shoulder, he shifts his weight. Then I hear a crunch.

That rascal is eating the cookie.

Around a mouthful, he says, "Mmm. It's good. Are you sure you don't want a bite?"

"Quite."

"Why are you so difficult?" he asks.

If I were standing, I'd swing at him. But I'm tired and feeling weak, my thoughts and vision remain a blur. Instead, I inwardly stagger as if that very question struck a blow. My voice is small when I answer, "Actually, I don't know."

Because I don't want help or handouts?

Because all my life I've been fighting?

Because the guy is trying to feed me?

That last one is ridiculous and brings to mind Mrs. Daley's conversation with me about the roof. My inner hunger amplifies because that day she served me sweet potato pie and sweet tea along with a hefty serving of the hard truth.

"Because every time I've taken a gamble on someone,

they've shown their real hand." My stomach sears with a gnawing hunger.

"Then maybe don't play cards with dishonest people."

The words hang between us. I can take them or leave them. It's my call.

Clearing my throat, I say, "I need real food."

As if knowing how hard this is for me, Maddock says, "This is just to tide you over. I'll make whatever you want. Name it. Chef Maddo at your service."

My thoughts turn fuzzy as my entire body turns slack in his arms.

Maddock tightens his grip. "Whoa there. Seriously, Honey. You need food."

"I know," I whisper.

As if we're a professional couples' dance pair, he somehow manages to sling me around so he's cradling me in his arms. After letting go of my legs, I slowly slide down his front as he sets me on my feet. He's at least six inches taller than me and I have to tip my head back slightly to meet his gaze.

Those deep blue eyes with the lighter ring around them hold on to me like a pair of life rings in a pool. I don't want to let go. Ever.

I rasp, "I don't know what I want to eat or why I refuse your help."

He nods as if understanding that I have some things that I need to work through.

I whisper, "But I do know that I get disappointed when your gaze looks anywhere but at me."

He shakes his head slowly. "I can hardly tear my eyes from you, Honey."

I tell myself not to blush, but as my cheeks turn pink, his smile grows, pleased to have this kind of effect on me.

Then, also, as if he knows what I'm craving, he says, "I'm

going to warm up Leonie's bottle and then you and I are having dinner."

Tallula's beignet buns are phenomenal and I take a few bites while Maddock makes Leonie's milk.

"The Laughing Gator Grille used to serve dinner, but I had to shorten opening hours. The Klatch is guaranteed early morning regulars, and since I'd often have an empty dining room at dinnertime, I cut the later hours." I list some of the old dinner menu items like gumbo, jambalaya, and crawfish étouffée. "Antoine still occasionally runs them as lunch specials."

"What was your favorite?"

"Lasagna."

Maddock does a double-take. "Wasn't expecting that on the menu."

"It wasn't. Cory's grandmother Nan made it once, and I fell in love." With the food and the boy.

Maddock swishes his lips from side to side. "Unfortunately, I don't have all the ingredients for lasagna, but I can scratch something together I think you'll like."

We sit on the porch and have pasta with meat sauce. Leonie sits in her bouncer-rocker combo seat between us, kicking her little feet. Both socks go flying.

Maddock sets his plate off to the side and wipes his mouth. "While I'm gone, you have to make me a promise."

"Only if you—" I'm about to tell him he can't get rid of the stuff from the chateau, but it's not like it's my stuff. Anything valuable is long gone. Mama, my cousin, and their cohorts were sure to take care of that. The problem is I don't want change. It's like if I hold on to things hard enough, nothing will slip through my fingers.

"Only if I what?" he asks.

Changing tact, I say, "Only if you promise to Facetime Leonie when you're free." She adores him.

He laughs. "That I'm more than happy to do."

The last of the sunlight flashes in his eyes and they catch hold of mine for a moment that burns through my defenses, seeps deep, and makes my heart swell.

We tag team the dinner clean up and the Leonie entertainment showcase. At some point, music comes on and the three of us dance in the kitchen. I have a moment where I imagine walking by the window and seeing this little family full of smiles and laughter. Only way out here, if someone were on the chateau property, they're definitely up to no good and we'd have to call the sheriff.

Thankfully, law enforcement isn't needed. Instead of the shadows of the past creeping back in, right now my heart is the fullest it's ever been. If I had a camera, I'd take a snapshot, capturing this moment in time.

After Leonie goes to sleep, I wander downstairs under the auspices of asking Maddock what he plans on doing with the truckload of stuff.

I find him stacking the boxes in the hallway closet.

"So you decided to keep it all?"

"Status pending. If after the renovation, you want to go through it all, you can decorate as you wish, open a museum, or sell it."

The idea of staying here, living here, teases me like a house of mirrors. "No yard sales, though. They attract scavengers."

"The scavenger hunters?"

"Same thing." I set the baby monitor on the table.

"But maybe someone will get lucky."

"Luck has nothing to do with it.

Maddock leans against the wall in the hallway and folds his arms in front of his chest. I feel like I'm staring down my own reckoning and sputter, "Hogan Tickle didn't intend for his riddles not to be solved."

"So if it's not luck, you mean someone smart will figure them out."

"Someone cunning. Cutthroat."

"Someone like you?"

Since living here, my sleep is much improved so my laughter isn't so much delirious as it is diabolical. It's my mother's laugh. I glance around, but she's not here. More like it echoes in this house.

Maddock's look at me is long and penetrating like he knows there's a chapter, the apex of the story, that I'm not sharing.

I keep my poker face.

"You don't think there's treasure, so what are people searching for?"

"Treasure."

"Now it sounds to me like you're the one speaking in riddles."

"Searching for treasure implies something valuable that was hidden. Seeking it consumes people and corrupts them. Makes them greedy. There's never enough."

"And you know this first hand?"

"Second hand. I'm not that kind of criminal." My shoulders lift and lower as I let out a breath, wondering how much I should tell Maddock. How much he can handle before he has second thoughts about coming back?

I sit down at the base of the stairs. A spot I've occupied many times, but never on this side of my life where there are genuine smiles, laughter, and something else that's just barely budding, but there nonetheless. Love.

Maddock steps closer, invading my space. Or did I invite him? The lines are blurring. Is that because I'm living at his house? This place is nearly as big as a hotel. We could go days without seeing each other if we wanted to. But we somehow always end up in the kitchen at the same time.

Maybe it's because we're both hungry for each other but are too stubborn to admit it.

"So are you going to tell me?" he asks, eyes dipping slightly in the direction of my mouth as if he's waiting to hear me speak the words ... or is it for something else?

"How good are you at keeping secrets?" I ask, feeling dangerously close to revealing mine.

# Chapter 14

## *Secret Treasure*

Ｉt's no surprise that Honey has secrets. They're hidden in the depths of her eyes. But it is a bit of a shock when she takes my hand in hers. I glance down as if worried the crocogator got ahold of me.

But it's just her calloused fingers in mine. She doesn't wear any jewelry ... maybe I'd like to change that even though I'm as far from admitting this as I will be from her come tomorrow.

But I don't want to think about distance with our hands linked.

Instead, I tighten my grip as if to tell Honey that I trust her to lead me wherever we're going.

We pass through the gathering room with the vandalized family tree and reach a narrow hall that dead ends. We pause in front of a painting of three men on horseback, disappearing into the sunset. It evokes a certain nostalgia for the old west and pioneer days, so I left it there. Honey reaches for it like she's going to tear it off the wall with one hand, but instead, I hear a click.

My eyebrows bounce as the painting opens on a hinge.

Wispy cobwebs fill half the opening, but it's big enough for someone my size to step through, so I follow Honey.

"You knew this was here?" I ask, my voice a dull echo.

"Of course." There are those words again. I wonder what else I'm going to learn tonight.

I cough from the dank, dusty air and would very much like my respirator and maybe my helmet just to be safe.

We turn right and the passage curves slightly.

"Are we behind the fireplace in the gathering room?"

"The office."

I picture the chateau's layout in my head, placing our location. "I thought I'd combed the house from top to bottom, but I didn't find this."

"You've hardly scratched the surface. Remember, Tickle ran with the Boot Beer Boys. He was a gambler too. That man kept no shortage of secrets, stashes, and stories that most would say are Hogwash."

"But not all," I say, picking up her meaning.

We stop again and without the aid of light, Honey manages to manipulate some levers into rotating the floor like the lazy Susan in my mother's spice cabinet. It opens to the dining room and we're standing where the China cabinet should be.

"Because all the fine China was gone, we didn't have to worry about making any noise," Honey says.

"Who's we?"

"*Les Trois Tasses*," she says in her Cajun French accent.

"My translation is a bit rusty, but *trois* means three in French, right?"

"*Oui.*" She nods.

"What about the rest?"

"It means The Three Cups. It was my cousin's idea. Like those shell games where something is hidden under one cup or shell, and the trickster shuffles them around, and then the player has to guess where the hidden object, usually their cash, went."

"Right into the trickster's pocket." Was the trickster Honey?

"Exactly." She crosses the room and gently taps the bar rail. The wainscoting pops open and she crouches down like she's done this dozens of times.

I drop to a squat. "*Trois*, three, so you, your cousin, and who was the third member?"

Honey glances at me before crawling through the opening. "My mother."

There's no way I'll fit so I go to the hall and into the next room, the parlor. She emerges where a long, moldering side table sat until recently. The marks are still visible on the floor.

"Mama and my cousin worked closely together, and I snuck in ..."

"Why them and not you and your mother?"

"My cousin was more willing. I didn't want anything to do with their schemes so they made me work in the shadows. The fact that I didn't want to be noticed helped. They were both quite noticeable, beautiful, boastful, show-women who loved the spotlight."

Honey is quietly beautiful, but not at all boastful, except when she wins at cards.

She stares out the window into the darkness. "Drunk in New Orleans like many sailors, my father wandered down the wrong street. There, he met a fortune teller. She told him he'd fall in love that night. At a bar two doors down, my mother was waiting. He was their mark after they noticed the gold watch." She shakes her head.

"Your mother and the fortune?"

"Her sister."

"That's some interesting matchmaking."

"They may have fallen ... in lust, but not love. I came along nine months later."

"And your father?"

"He denies that I'm his. My mother wasn't particularly honest, but I knew it was him. We have the same eyes."

My heart does something funny and I listen for the baby monitor, but Leonie is fast asleep upstairs.

"And you ended up here?"

"At some point, Mama heard about Tickle's Golden Tokens and joined the hunt."

Honey sits down at the table and pulls a deck of cards out of a hidden compartment. She shuffles, then deals, while explaining, "Hogwash Holler draws treasure hunters. It was once home to roadside attractions, including the world's smallest chicken coop ... and the largest one. A massive nest made entirely of peacock feathers collected from within our town limits, and of course the giant rotating mug of root beer."

"And a crocogator."

Her lips pucker with laughter as she deals.

I reveal my cards, having lost, and say, "Sounds like a lot of tall tales."

"I've seen the crocogator."

I arch an eyebrow. "Back to Tickle's Golden Tokens ..."

"Which don't lead to treasure. Only to people fighting to get it. The quest ruined families. The town too." She deals again.

I look carefully over my cards, not wanting to miss a trick. "I'd like to fix that."

"But you can't fix people, Maddock. The women in my family were as crafty as they come. They exploited the desires of the scavenger hunters, the people seeking Tickle's Golden Tokens. We'd clean 'em out. When I finally turned eighteen, I got out. But it came with a price." She goes suddenly quiet as if she's afraid she said too much.

My brow furrows because I can see why she wants to let go of the past but not of control.

The gauzy curtains swish like ghosts trying to escape the truth. It's eerie here at night, especially when the misty fog settles over the bayou beyond the windows. I don't love the idea of leaving Honey here alone, but if she's anything like the other *Les Trois Tasses*, she can outwit a ghost or walk into the darkest night and challenge anything to spook her.

"You talk about them in the past tense."

"Mama is in jail. My cousin disappeared. Probably conned some poor guy into marrying her—well, a rich guy because she wouldn't settle for anything less." With a smile, Honey reveals her cards. Again, she wins and starts dealing again.

"Where'd you learn to play?"

"I was my mother's protégé. I spent the first half of my childhood on gambling riverboats. Mama was part of the entertainment but didn't get paid much. Though, by the time we made landing, she'd have enough for that month's living expenses." The expression Honey gives suggests she was robbing the gullible people on the cruise.

It's then that I realize that my wrist is bare. Honey dangles my grandfather's military field watch from her forefinger.

Eyes bulging, I reach for it. "It's not worth much."

"But it holds sentimental value. Something's worth isn't always measured in money." Honey's smile slips toward sadness and makes me wonder if her mother using her in this parlor played into her sense of self-worth.

I pat my pockets. "I'll take my wallet too. Nice sleight of hand. Deal again."

She returns my watch and deals the cards.

Determined to win, I absently ask, "So how does the Porsche tie into this? Was it your final, big score?"

"Don't make it sound as if I enjoyed any of it. I despised what we did. Myself too."

"I'm sorry. I didn't mean it that way."

She nods. "The car—" She opens and closes her mouth like she debates whether to say more. "Before we started the gig here at the chateau, we ran in New Orleans. As soon as I was tall enough to reach a car's pedals, I became the getaway driver."

My jaw lowers.

"I was good at driving. A natural, people said. Then one day I drove right into Cory Peterson."

"You ran someone over?"

"No. Technically, he drove into me. Crashed." She demonstrates with her hands as she arrays her cards. Final hand. Winning hand.

Funny that's how we met, though thankfully without any auto damage, then I make the connection to Cory's shop in town.

I fold, dropping my cards on the table. "You're good."

"Too good. At least that's what Mama said. She named me Honey because I was the only sweet thing in her life. I didn't want mine to turn out like hers. Cory was my oasis. He liked to drive too. We'd race. Me to escape the fact that I'd likely turn out to be a felon. He because of the adrenaline." Once more, she goes quiet as if that's the end of the story.

"Were you, him, and Jesse the new *Three Amigos*?"

"Not even close. Jesse grew up more like me. Cory was one of the good ones." Her chin quivers. She gets to her feet and says, "I should check on Leonie."

I follow her to the living room with the baby monitor. Had

she made a peep, we would've heard it from the parlor, but I think Honey needs a moment.

"Cory and I were close," she says softly.

I get the sense they were sweethearts though she might not phrase it that way.

"He joined the military. Died—unrelated. That's JQ's story to tell. Losing him was the first thing that woke me up."

"Was there a second?"

"And a third. The second was Mama going to prison for a long, long time. I thought it would set straight my cousin too, but no such luck."

"And the third?"

"There I was minding my own business when an infant turned up on my doorstep. Okay, I wasn't minding my business exactly. Living in this small southern town my whole life, it's hard not to catch a whiff of gossip—or be the focus of it."

"Do you know who's baby she is?"

"My cousin. She never made an honest wager."

"It was good of you to take care of Leonie."

"I wouldn't have it any other way. But what else can I expect? Tragedy trails me like a stray cat. Can't seem to shake the travesties either. But she's a treasure, so it's worked out okay."

"What about lost things?" I ask.

"Do you mean the Cahoot Ruby and the Dubois Diamond?"

"And Tickle's Golden Tokens."

"All I can say about that is good luck." She tips her head as if trying to talk herself into or out of something. She gazes down at her hands and then up at me. "Maddock, I'm not equipped to deal with a relationship."

"You've figured out motherhood."

"Hardly."

"Give yourself more credit."

Her voice is thick when she says, "I'm figuring it out as I go."

Story of my life. "While you've been at the restaurant, I've been learning about Hugwash."

"Hogwash."

"Sounds the same to me."

We exchange a smile.

I continue, "Recently, an anonymous donor pledged funds to repair and maintain the community center for the next hundred years."

"That's generous."

"According to the bank records, they paid in gold."

Honey's eyes light up. "Is that so?"

I nod slowly. "That it is."

Then as if having doubts, she says, "Remember, this is Hogwash Holler. Don't believe everything you hear."

"But I do believe my eyes. I saw the financial transaction receipt. I also see the history books ... and the way you look at me."

She bunches her lips together. "Oh yeah. How's that?"

"You like me." My thoughts float to our first tour of the estate property.

"And you think I've finally realized it?"

My grin reaches my eyes because I know it's true even if she goes on denying it.

"You are so cocky."

"I prefer to think of it as confident. But you are so right."

She tilts her head at a *Did I just hear what I think I heard?* angle. "You admit that I'm right about something." Then her jaw lowers and her eyes narrow, shining on me, for me. "You just tricked me."

I can't help my gloating laughter, but I keep it playful and light.

Honey pokes me in the chest with each word she speaks. "You. Are. Going. To. Regret. This."

I wrap my fingers around hers and draw her hand close to my face, contemplating where to start, not wanting to think about it ending.

My tone is gravelly when I say, "You're wrong about that."

Her jaw lowers and she tries to bite her lip, but it slips from her teeth.

"Shocked by my audacity?" I ask.

"Floored."

But this is where our disagreement stops and the space between us narrows.

I search her brown eyes. Our proximity strikes a match in them.

"I'm not sure I can fight this fire." My voice breaks.

What has felt tense, dark, and impenetrable yields as her eyes flick to mine. She knows we're on a crash course and does nothing to stop it.

I don't either. No, I accelerate it.

Leyton once told me that only fools rush into unknown situations. His constant drilling to *Stop Assess Act* flashes in my mind now. But I ignore it because I'm a fool for this woman, and I want to rush in.

Our mouths meet with fervor, greed, and hunger. It's like we've been staving this off, starving for each other, and now the banquet table is set. The feast begins and we're stuffing ourselves silly as our breathing comes hard and fast and our motions erratic and frenzied.

My hands are all over Honey. She works hard and her palms have calluses, but everything else about her is soft, supple, and sweet. Her hair is silkier than I imagined … and I've thought about it more than I dare admit.

Her hands cover a lot of surface area, sliding up the sides of my neck, gripping my jaw, cascading down my back, and holding me tight.

This woman is so much more than I deserve. More than I could hope for. She meets me where I am and makes me better. Yes, I even want to kiss her better than I've ever kissed anyone. Give her more than I've ever given anyone.

Her breath is warm against my cheek as I nibble the spot behind her ear, pausing because I'm struggling to catch mine. She takes it away from me but gives me so much more.

The tiny hairs loose around her neck tickle my cheek. I laugh a little.

She draws back. Her eyes sparkle, but her brow furrows.

I say, "This is so unexpected yet so right."

"No, Maddo. It was inevitable."

I don't argue because I agree.

Her hands grip the back of my neck, returning my mouth to hers. It's as if she doesn't want to let me go anywhere. And I don't. I'm rethinking my plan. My entire life plan. Because I want Honey to be in it. I want her and a future I never foresaw for myself. It's even better than a Plan B. Better than all the plans. I want to see where this goes if she'll let me.

Everything about Honey is sweet except for pieces of her past and her side of sass. But I'll take it. Double portions, please.

The kiss deepens and this is all I want. All I need.

# Chapter 15

## *Ew. Gross*

**M**addock pulls back slightly, breaking the kiss. His blue eyes capture mine with a question.

In response, I say the reasonable thing, "We probably shouldn't be doing this."

"But do we want to?" His voice is low, saturated with honey.

I'm afraid I'm developing feelings. That we're falling ... together and this is just the beginning. But I don't dare reveal that.

I say, "This is probably a bad idea."

The flame in his eyes tells me he disagrees. The one in my belly burning me up suggests I'm lying to myself.

"Don't tell me you haven't been thinking about this every day since we talked about not kissing."

Every hour of every day. But instead, I say, "You know as well as I do. There are strings."

"Maybe I like these particular strings. Maybe I want strings in my life."

"I find that hard to believe given the way you roared into town."

He leans in and roars in my ear, then whispers, "I think you secretly like it." Again, he nibble-kisses the spot behind my ear and I melt.

But before the world turns totally fuzzy, I say, "I'm afraid to have this conversation because of what it could mean or result in. Not because I don't want it, but because I don't trust it. It's easier to tell you off than to let you in."

He leans back and goes still. "Is it?"

I nod slowly and he searches my eyes. His gaze alone fills me up in a way that I didn't realize I needed or wanted, but the risk freezes me in place.

Maddock's rough fingers trace my jawline and his thumb rubs my chin. "I want my lips on yours. I want your mouth on mine. But I'll wait until you're ready."

It's been a long time since someone has been considerate of me in this way. But that almost makes it worse. Makes me want him more.

So I drop my lead foot on the gas and go.

I cannot hold back. Fisting his shirt in my hand, I tug him toward me. Once more, we're kissing and his hands on my skin ignite me.

Maddock lets me direct the proximity and intensity. The space between us narrows until it no longer exists. My hands grip his back as if I'm holding on for dear life. Some days it feels like I'm falling. All over my failures. But this is something else. It's a different kind of falling ... more like I'm floating. However, I'm not in a fog. More like a daze as my thoughts drift away, leaving nothing other than affection and sensation as Maddock slides his fingers through my hair.

As the kiss deepens, his pulse is erratic, yet somehow mine remains steady. With this man, it's like I can breathe again.

But this is risky. What if I come to rely on it? What if he leaves?

Right now, with his mouth on mine and his big, warm, protective body pressing against me, I decide to let myself forget until tomorrow. This is my first time kissing Maddock and with him leaving, I fear it could be our last as well. So I pour myself into it, never wanting it to end.

**\* \* \***

Shooting upright in bed, I wake with a start. I have the eerie feeling someone is watching me sleep. But I was also having a bad dream. After nearly baring my soul to Maddock last night, the secrets that I usually keep under lock and key snuck loose.

Well, most of them.

Fitting that it's the day before Halloween, traditionally the night that young, misguided youths do things like toilet paper houses, toss eggs at cars, and other unruly things. I'm not saying I didn't partake, but I'm not *not* saying that either.

Leonie rouses in the Pack 'n Play and I recommit myself to her life never resembling the one I recounted last night. I won't drag her into debauchery or debacles, use her as an accomplice or exit strategy as my mother did.

Taking the little bundle of love into my arms, I sing our morning sunshine wake-up song. As I pass the window, Maddock's truck disappears under the canopy of trees down Shady Lane.

I never imagined my life would take me back here in such an unexpected and somewhat redemptive way. I want to hate this house with its many rooms, secret passageways, and memories, but I can't hate anything with Leonie's bright blue eyes looking around with wonder.

It's my day off, which is another way of saying the day to do all the things I can't manage while running the restaurant during the work week. This includes, but is not limited to laundry, bills, and other responsibilities that I sometimes avoid. Not because I'm lazy or negligent. More because I rarely have the cash to pay for things like insurance for the mobile home, but I figured I could skip a couple of months given the new roof. If I have the chance to go over to Sunnyside today, I should probably check on things, grab some more clothes, and see if there's anything salvageable—if rodents haven't kicked out the frogs and made themselves at home.

When Leonie and I get downstairs, I find five days' worth of breakfast treats on the counter—muffins, pastries, and beignet buns—along with coffee and a note that says, *Don't you dare eat any of this! xo Maddock.*

I chuckle at his calling me out on my stubbornness by trying reverse psychology. I'm onto him ... and really into him, as it turns out. I cannot erase the kiss from last night from my mind. I don't want to. But the little thrills that shoot through me when I remember the heat of his hands on my skin, the spark between our lips, and the fire in his eyes is like living in a daydream.

When I get the baby's milk from the fridge, I discover that it's stocked with labeled glass containers. Another note from Maddock includes reheating instructions. He provided a week's worth of meals so I don't get caught up and miss a meal. My jaw hangs open.

No one has ever done something so ... thoughtful.

If I could afford to hire an employee besides Antoine to pay in cash rather than crème brûlée, then I wouldn't be running myself ragged. But Maddock's meal gesture touches a place inside I'd cordoned off, fueling me in the best of ways.

After Leonie and I have breakfast, we walk over to the mobile home park. It's a beautiful fall day. The air is crisp for southern Louisiana and the leaves have faded to shades of yellow and gold. They carpet Shady Lane and I sing the "Yellow Brick Road" song to Leonie. She giggles all the way.

The electric company cleared out the fallen tree and debris, but the fact of the matter is my trailer is in shambles. Granted, it wasn't in great shape to begin with, but now it's an absolute dump. Already soggy from the storm, I'm not going to add my tears to the mess, but frustration builds. Feelings of helplessness tie me in knots. If it weren't for Maddock's generosity, we'd be living in the office in the restaurant. I don't like the feeling of being in someone's debt. I have enough of that as it is.

Still standing outside, the crunch of tires over gravel startles me. It's Jesse, but he's in his regular truck.

"Howdy," he calls with a tip of his hat.

Tallula hops out of the passenger side. We swap a hug and she takes Leonie with glee. Lexi and JQ aren't the only ones who will soon be starting a family.

"It's remarkable," he says.

"That a power line came loose during the storm, the pole got hung up in my favorite magnolia tree, and the whole thing came crashing down on my house?"

"That, but also that Maddock was the one who took charge and prevented a major fire and possibly injury to our local crew."

It's also pretty amazing how quickly he cleaned up the estate—granted, it's not in any shape to be featured in an HLTV special, but it's livable, whereas this place is ready for a Dumpster ... and how he did laundry, including a bunch of his T-shirts, has been helping take care of Leonie, and keeping me well supplied with snacks and meals.

"I saw you over here and figured if you were thinking of heading inside, we'd go together."

"That's mighty nice of you, Jesse, but—"

He shakes his head. "No arguing. These are Maddock's instructions. As it is, the place is a hazard, but likely you want to retrieve some of your things."

He's right, so I accept this help while Tallula entertains Leonie. We pick through the debris, but there's not much worth salvaging. Just some clothes, a few mementos, and kitchen items.

Once back outside, Leonie lets out her little lion roar when she spots me. I take her and a pile of mail from Tallula grabbed from the overflowing mailbox.

She says, "You have to come by the Coffee Loft to grab a complimentary baked good every day starting next week."

"Tallula, you don't have to—" I'm about to decline her offer.

"Maddock took care of it." She bites her lip as if sensing I might not like Maddock using her as a conduit to bark commands.

Fine. Secretly, I love it. I've never been taken care of like this. It makes me feel twitchy, but also something else ...

"Well, thank you."

She clears her throat. "He also said that if you don't follow orders, there will be consequences."

I'd cross my arms in front of my chest, but they're full of mail—which I could do without—and Leonie, who's being a major snuggler right now.

After we say goodbye, we walk back down the tree-covered lane to the chateau. Tire tracks lead onward toward the cemetery and fort. It's too early for Hogwash Hunters to be out this way. Perhaps, in addition to making sure that I'll be fed and watered daily, Maddock took a spin down there before he left.

The big house stands imposing before us, but it's far less haunted looking than when I brought Maddock here for the first time—he let a lot of little light into this place and my life.

Leonie looks around and I point out things we pass—a

squirrel, a daisy, and a maple tree. From the nearby bayou, a twig snaps and a bird caws as it flies skyward. The only wildlife I have a real concern about are gators, including the crocogator, so I hustle inside.

When Leonie goes down for her nap, I pick through my mail, sorting bills from junk. Letters from my mother go in that pile, too.

Unfortunately, for Luckie, it's too little too late. I'm not interested in her wild theories or get-rich-quick schemes. Instead of the depressing state of my finances, I set aside the stack and pick through the cupboards. Yes, I serve pancakes every day at the restaurant, but I could go for a fluffy stack with butter and syrup right now.

While looking for a whisk, I find the old cookbook with the red fabric cover worn thin by use in a drawer. I'd forgotten all about it. On the inside, it says, *Property of Eloise Tickle.*

The paper bound by three rings is brittle and I turn them carefully. It contains handwritten recipes along with others meticulously cut out from newspapers and magazines. Notes about variations, measurements, and personalizations fill the margins. Tickle was a big fan of the flapjacks with a side of mulberries when in season. I grunt because Maddock would probably like them, too.

So many people came through this old house—from my mother with her schemes and scams, Jesse and Sawyer with their spray paint, and countless others looking for treasure. "Yet they missed this," I whisper.

Sure, it might not be valuable to some, but inspiration sparks as I review the recipes, including sweet potato hash, one for a roast with rosemary, okra salad, chocolate pudding, and an apple tart. At some point, I will update the menu at the restaurant and add some of these.

When I reach the back, there are some kid-friendly recipes

too, including one for "Baby's First Birthday Cake," along with finger foods and a secret ingredient pasta sauce to "Ensure Nutrition." Spoiler alert: it involves pureed collard greens.

That night, after Leonie goes to sleep, I take the cookbook upstairs with me to bed and make a list of recipes to try. Maybe I can make some of them for Maddock, yes, including the flapjacks.

The memory of us in the dusty secret passages, him keeping close to me, and the warmth he radiates prompts me to kick off the bedspread. Being so close to him made me feel heady.

All those times I found his gaze straying to me made me feel like I was in the spotlight—a place I avoided, unlike others in my family. But then I was disappointed when he didn't look, which must mean something.

I don't want to tell him that he was right, that I do like him but just didn't realize it. I sure liked our kiss. And I'm rather fond of his deep voice. The way he can't keep his eyes—or hands—off me. I'm a fan of the flannel and the firefighter command in his stature and composure. He's a protector and maybe I needed rescuing. From the state of my life, but also parts of myself. Perhaps he met his match with me and I popped his big-headed balloon of arrogance so he could join the rest of us here on solid ground.

A creaking sound comes from somewhere in the house, but I mostly ignore the old sounds it makes. It must be settling with the weather change as the seasons shift closer to winter. Southern winter, but still. Don't be fooled, it gets cooler here, relatively speaking.

I take a photo of the flapjack recipe and send it to Maddock in a text. It's earlier on the West Coast and he's probably working, but maybe he'd like to know that I'm thinking of him.

Me: These will be waiting for you when you get back.

He replies less than a minute later.

Maddock: Will you be, too?

# Chapter 16

## *Gone West*

I'm leading the wildland firefighter training for our new crew stationed between Carson City and Reno. Primarily, they'll be responding to calls from city folk who're visiting Tahoe, don't have four-wheel or all-wheel drive, and get stranded. But from time to time, there are real disasters and these guys will be called to the line.

I've been there plenty of times, always the one out front, who volunteered to do extra, or the things the others avoided—latrine duty, anyone? My hand would go up. The point was to be disciplined enough to learn. But over time, with that came some bravado because even if I didn't know what to do, I'd still answer the call. This is why I was surprised Leyton picked me to teach.

A few nights ago, he said he wanted me here because, for some guys, that level of commitment to learning leads to being intuitive. Or they just get stuck being brash boneheads. I guess I'm one of the lucky ones because even though I'll still be the first to try to mitigate danger, my brazen—some would say cocky—behavior burned up. Extinguished. Could be because I no longer feel like I have something to prove. Truth is, I only care about what a woman down in Hogwash thinks of me.

I missed these mountains, but I miss Honey and Leonie more. I'll take the muggy air and mosquitos and the bayou if it means I get them too. Even though the crew has me busy, I look forward to our daily text exchanges. Sometimes hourly. We've video-called a few times as well.

Honey sends me a daily photo of her and Leonie. I'm not exactly the sentimental type, but this would make for a few pages in a scrapbook. The caption would be about our time apart and then the rest of the photos would be of our happy reunion.

Trust me, I'm counting down the days until I can make silly faces at Leonie and listen to her laugh. Have my morning cup of coffee with Honey, make dinner for us, and watch the transformation at the chateau.

Also, I'm especially excited to kiss Honey again. Her soft yet hungry lips on mine were unlike anything I'd ever experienced. Forget messing up my pulse, I'm a living, breathing, roaring five-alarm fire. I'm not sure there's anything left of the old me and I don't mind.

It's odd how I went to Hogwash Holler thinking I'd run the town into the ground in an act of revenge against my ex, to make her look bad and regret all of her life's decisions. Instead, I potentially got a family out of the deal.

At least, I hope so.

My phone beeps. It's a few hours later in Louisiana than it is here, so Leonie is probably asleep which means we can talk, er, text.

> Honey: I keep hearing things outside. If I didn't know better, I'd think the crocogator has a posse and they're partying in the woods.

Me: Lexi and JQ warned me about swamp zombies.

Honey: I just laughed out loud and almost woke up Leonie. Jesse and I made that up to keep everyone away from Shady Lane.

Me: So you could find the treasure?

Honey: We weren't that dumb. Okay, we were. But I still don't think it's there, er, here.

Me: But other people do.

I belatedly realize suggesting that someone is out there might frighten Honey. Then again, nothing scares her. The woman is unshakeable. I wish I weren't so far away. Even though she's tough, I like the idea that she'd turn to me for safety and security.

Honey: It's too early for the Hogwash Hunt.

Me: Pirates aren't known for following the rules.

Honey: You mean scavenger hunters?

Me: When should we expect them?

Honey: The Hogwash Hunt begins January 2, but more importantly, when can we expect you?

Me: Are you saying you want me?

Our back and forth is usually pretty snappy when Leonie is asleep and I'm off the clock. However, the little texting dots blink for longer than usual, like Honey is trying to figure out how to respond.

> Honey: I want reliability.

> Honey: I want integrity.

> Honey: I want honesty.

> Honey: I want your mouth on mine.

> Honey: Does that answer your question?

Yes, very much so. I shift slightly, suddenly hot and I clear my throat.

> Me: Don't miss me too much.

> Honey: Leonie keeps me distracted. And these noises.

I open a browser window on my phone and look up a security system company in the area, wishing I'd done this sooner. I make a call and pay extra for the technicians to go to the chateau tomorrow.

> Me: It's probably the cat.

> Honey: Minou is curled up at the end of the bed.

I'll admit that I wish I was, even though Honey won't let me into the bedroom. I'd settle for the couch, with her head on my shoulder or even taking a walk and holding hands.

> Me: Workers from SecuriTech will be at the house at eight. I told them to swing by the restaurant to grab the key from you.

> Honey: You're having a security system installed?

> Me: Since Flap and Jack are all the way on the other side of the country, I can't be your bodyguard, so yeah.

> Honey: Are you calling your arm muscles Flap and Jack? I think we can do better than that.

> Me: Flapjack? Better than Pan and Cake ... or we could just go with hotcakes.

I add the winking face. I can't help it, even though I take Honey and Leonie's safety seriously, I'm smiling because this woman just gets me. And I get her.

> Me: Yep. Flap and Jack miss you. They want to make sure you're safe until they can hold you in their arms again.

> Honey: Are you saying you want me?

My grin grows and one of the guys across the room snickers as if he knows I'm messaging someone special. Can't let them see my soft side, so I go outside onto the deck overlooking Carson Spur, part of the Sierra Nevada range, dotted with evergreen stubble as it slopes gently toward meadowlands.

I flip through a few of the recent photos of Leonie and get to some that include Honey. My heart melts as I look at the baby with her bright blue eyes. But my pulse picks up the pace and goes wild when I look at Honey with her steady yet sparkling gaze. The woman has known mischief and isn't afraid to stand up for herself—or stand by the people she loves, namely her little girl. She's strong, thoughtful, and resilient, and the kind of woman a guy would never regret.

There is no other way to answer her question so I keep it simple.

> **Me: Yes, I want you.**

> **Me: I want you bad.**

It only gets worse as the days that we're apart turn into weeks. Thanksgiving is an over-the-top affair at the fire crew school house with a fried turkey, a roasted turkey, and a smoked turkey, plus all the fixings. However, someone forgot to add the marshmallows to the sweet potatoes. I think it's a crime, and among the guys, a serious debate ensues. I'll have to ask Honey her take, leaving me longing to be around the table in Hogwash with her and Leonie.

Leyton makes us go around and tell everyone something we're thankful for. Following his cue, I keep it short and tell the guys I appreciate this opportunity to teach them and see them grow as firefighters.

The part I keep to myself is that I'm grateful that in the divorce settlement with my ex-wife, I inherited a town. I see so much potential there from the quaint main street to making everything at the end of Shady Lane into a home and a historic site where visitors can enjoy the old legends rather than leaving the place in ruin in search of treasure.

In my downtime, when I'm not connecting with Honey or hiking, I've been researching the history of Cameron Parish, Hogwash, and the Hunt in particular.

I wonder if there is a way to call it off while commemorating it at the same time. Then again, I don't think anyone will give up hope on discovering Tickle's Tokens until they're all recovered.

Before I left, JQ confided in me. He said since I own the town, I ought to know. The Tokens are real. He and Lexi found one ... and some other stuff. I'm pretty sure they're behind funding the refurbishment of the community center and swimming pool.

Teaching Leonie to swim—and water safety, of course, we deal with a lot of that in my profession—makes me grin. Also, I wouldn't object to seeing Honey in a bathing suit.

My phone beeps as if she's reading my mind, but it's a message from one of the parish administrators about the updated plat for the estate property. Some years ago, someone petitioned for the land to be split, possibly for development. As it stands, the estate, cemetery, and another section which looks like it includes two other structures remain intact. The Fort is state property, but the Tickle Estate, which hadn't been assigned to anyone until I came along, has access and other rights. However, numerous people over the years laid claim to being a descendent.

Thankfully, they were denied.

If we can find the tokens, we can turn the scavenger hunters into civilized guests. Maybe Hogwash could become a vacation destination—one of those quaint coastal towns featured on social media. I love the idea of Honey and Leonie— maybe more kids—someday filling those rooms, but it would also make a good boutique hotel. The Fort could be a point of interest and we could open the area up with a waterfront for airboat rides. I'm getting ahead of myself, but the idea and inspiration won't quit.

When I get back to Hogwash, I plan to tell Honey. However, I haven't figured out how to convince her the Tokens are real without betraying JQ.

Then again, she and I shouldn't keep secrets. I know Honey still has a few.

* * *

It's December first, and my countdown is officially on. I'll be leaving here on December twenty-first and driving east each day until I run out of gas—figuratively speaking.

My phone beeps.

> Honey: I have good news. Well, more of a surprise.

Before I can read the next message, Leyton and the others snag my attention. I have to get out to the field for the practical hands-on portion of the program. My phone vibrates a few more times while I review rangeland fire mitigation tactics with the students. I try not to let curiosity about the message distract me.

Maybe Leonie got her first tooth—Honey says she senses teething even though it's a little on the early side. At night, I've been reading chapters in "It's a Baby's World: We Just Live in It." The inch-thick tome is about what to expect from conception to twenty-four months.

Or maybe Honey perfected the apple tart she's been working on from Eloise Tickle's cookbook. She's mentioned updating the Laughing Gator Grille menu in the new year. Her pancakes are the best I've ever had even though I won't give her the pleasure of calling them anything but flapjacks.

Could be that Mrs. Halfpenny realized her dog requires batteries or Molly is finally pronouncing crème brûlée properly.

When one of the students answers a question I pose about

evergreen sap's flammability, I realize Honey must've gotten a Christmas tree.

At lunchtime, I finally have a chance to see what Honey has to say and the message string is long on her side. The most recent one demands to know whether I consider *Die Hard* a Christmas movie.

I go outside and call her directly.

"What's going on?"

She answers on the second to last ring. "I can't talk much right now. Jesse is here investigating. It doesn't look like anything was taken except for a bunch of biscuits."

"Slow down. Last I heard, you wanted to know my thoughts on Die Hard. Obviously, it's a Christmas movie."

"But since then, someone broke into the Laughing Gator Grille and made a mess of my Christmas decorations." Her voice is strained.

"Are you okay?"

"Of course. This is me we're talking about." True. Had she been at the restaurant, she'd have fought them off with a frying pan.

"Any idea who or why?"

"Swamp zombies?" she says thinly.

A rash of heat breaks out across my skin because I'm here and she's there, and there's not a thing I can do. Honey is strong but rattled and I hate that.

Thinking fast, I say, "I'll have SecuriTech outfit the restaurant by the end of the week."

"You can't do that."

"Careful with those words, Honey," I say, my voice sharper than I mean because if she dares to try to push me away when it comes to her safety, I will mow down Hogwash and anyone who so much as touches a hair on her head—or a potato in her restaurant.

.

171

"I thought maybe it could've been Roxy and Sawyer again, given the fact they were behind the stolen rotating root beer mug. But Jesse thinks it has something to do with the Hunt."

I nod, recalling our conversation a few weeks ago when she heard noises outside the chateau.

"Could be early bird scavengers."

"Well, they'd better watch out ... no one has found Chick Jagger. If I'm not mistaken, the mayor is a bird and the crocogator is on the loose."

She laughs faintly.

"Is Leonie okay?"

"She's with Lexi today."

"How about you?" I ask to give her a chance to lean on me if she needs to.

"You know me."

"What was your good news from earlier?" I ask, following up with an apology for not being able to reply.

"I think I'll let it be a surprise."

I eye my truck parked in the gravel lot, eager for the next three weeks to fly by.

Thankfully, they do without incident—well, there was Couger in the kitchen with the squash soufflé. Thankfully, we're equipped with fire extinguishers, fire blankets, and baking soda in a pinch. Kids, do not try this at home.

They call him Couger because he's the youngest on the team, yet the older ladies seem to love him anytime we go to town. Fitting he'd make soufflé which seems like it would be a hit with the silver-haired set. No offense to anyone. I found a couple of grays on my head the other day.

Eggs remind me of chickens which makes me think of Hogwash's supposed mayor. As the owner of the town, according to parish statutes, I'm not eligible to take on that role, but that begs the question: How was a rooster voted in?

Maybe his hens lay golden eggs.

It's then I know what I'm going to get Leonie and Honey for Christmas.

The last time we video call before I hit the road, I tease her with hints about my gifts. Her expression falters and I remember she's not great at receiving things from other people. But this one, she'll love.

"Well, I still have a surprise for you when you get back. Bring an appetite."

"Oh, I will ... and not just for flapjacks." I wink and then end the call because the truck is gassed up and I'm bound and determined to get to Hogwash by Christmas.

# Chapter 17

## Deck the Walls

Is it weird that I'm nervous about Maddock coming home? If I were a normal person, no, not at all. Having butterflies about a guy is perfectly acceptable.

But I'm me. Honey Hamilton. Pancake Queen and Independent Girl Boss.

But that's just it.

All this time, I've been thinking like a girl and not a woman. A mature adult would realize that it's okay to sometimes ask for help and receive it. I can be strong but don't need to seize and hold on to my so-called independence with a death grip at the cost of relationships with people who truly want to help. Meanwhile, I've been pushing everyone away or making them feel bad about their generosity.

I'm not generally one to make New Year's resolutions, but I have a list already and it includes being a better recipient of people's kindness. As soon as the restaurant gets out of the red, I plan on hosting a big 'ole crawfish foodie fry like the Guidrys used to do before George and Lucille started playing cards with my mother.

But first, Christmas.

Before the storm that moved Leonie and me into this house, Maddock had done a decent job ridding the chateau of dust and grime. Aside from me rescuing those boxes he was going to donate, anything moldering or covered in mildew was brought to the landfill.

However, a couple of weeks ago, I heard a suspicious sound from downstairs. With a frying pan in hand in case I needed to defend myself, I uncovered Minou clawing at the wall. Chances are we have a rodent problem rather than an intruder, but I'll let Maddock deal with that when he gets here.

The next morning, she was still at it and had left scratch marks all over the wood baseboard. When I tried to rub them out, a strip of beveled baseboard indented like a piano key. I uncovered another secret built into this house.

After fiddling with it, pulling, pushing, and twisting, I realized it was a latch and opened a little hatch in the wall. Inside was barely a crawlspace, but reaching inside like the scene in Indiana Jones and the Temple of Doom, instead of bugs and creepy crawlies, I discovered a cache of Christmas decorations.

However, I still can't figure out how to get to it because it's so small—big enough for a cat or a bunny to crawl through. I don't know if someone plastered over a larger opening or how they got in there, but I've been trying to puzzle out how to get them out without using a sledgehammer.

In Louisiana, it's rare for houses, even chateaus, to have a basement so I can't go under. Given my experience in the secret passages of this house, none of them lead to the Christmas treasure in that particular spot.

With Maddock on his way, I'm desperate to dig them out because the good news I was going to share with him was that I got a Christmas tree—but my decorations were destroyed in the storm. I wanted to surprise him by having the chateau decorated for the holidays, but with the clock ticking and my bank account barely covering the restaurant expenses this month, I can't head over to the This & That for holiday décor, not even at a rock bottom bargain.

Especially not when I know there is a huge vintage collection buried in the wall. It's been bothering me and short of demolition, I'm at a loss for what to do.

Yes, I'm obsessed because the clock is ticking.

During Leonie's bath, I make up a silly song about how she's going to see Maddock the next day. My rhymes are terrible, but I almost refer to him as *Daddy* twice because it kind of rhymes with happy.

I abruptly go quiet, startled by the notion while she kicks her feet and smiles. Her face turns serious in my silence. I change the word to *crawdaddy*, which is even less of a rhyme.

"What is wrong with me?" I ask in nearly a whisper.

The truth settles on the surface like the bubbles in the baby tub. Part of me wishes that Maddock was Leonie's father—that we were a family.

"Who am I and what happened to Honey?" I ask, my voice barely above a whisper.

Leonie roars with joy and claps her hands together.

"I'm your mommy, that's who," I say, continuing her bath and my silly song.

After bedtime, I decide to make one last attempt at getting to the Christmas decorations. I imagine Eloise put them there, but how? If I were a well-to-do housewife in the early twentieth century with a penchant for pie and porcelain pigs, why would I hide my Christmas decorations in the wall? I learned about the pie from her cookbook and the pigs when I found some from her collection back in the day when I'd sneak around at my mother's behest.

The answer escapes me ... unless she didn't hide the decorations. Maybe it was Hogan.

Questions circle my mind like the sugarplums dancing in Leonie's dreams.

There is a chance that Hogan stashed them after his wife's passing. Maybe the decorations were a difficult reminder of losing Eloise. To a lesser degree, I know the feeling.

I keep most thoughts about Cory under lock and key. Even though we weren't married, up until he left for military service, I thought he was the one. Maddock and I met in much the same way. Only, we didn't damage each other's cars. Maybe this bodes well for us ... for me to have a second chance at true love.

As I pad through the quiet house, filled with old memories and antiques and mixed with our newer belongings, I realize that I've been living in the past and telling myself I wasn't hurt while fighting against the present because I've carried all that pain and loss with me.

Time to let go, no?

Maybe Hogan had a similar thought and the only way for him to do so was to hide it out of sight. He must've known every inch, secret space, and passage in this place. I catalog what I know about him and repeatedly return to gambling. But that can't have anything to do with Christmas decorations, can it?

Given the notes in the cookbook, he had a big appetite and enjoyed Eloise's chicken pot pie, corn fritters, and apple tart. But he liked gambling more.

I repeatedly return to this and question whether it's stuck in my craw because of my mother or for some other reason. But what?

Awash in thought, I pad from the parlor to the dining room with the rotating shelf before arriving in the hall off the gathering room.

It's a cool night and the chateau is drafty. Maddock's

improvements were mainly cosmetic, but if he—er, we?—plan to live here, we'll need some insulation and new windows. The curtains move, making me think of ghosts.

I whisper, "This place isn't haunted."

As if in response, the wind blows a long *oooooooh* outside.

Spooked, my goosebumps turn into ghoul-bumps. At this rate, I won't be able to fall asleep. I could be restless in bed, wondering or I could check one last thing ...

Preparing myself with a deep breath, once in the secret passage, I shine my cell phone's light up, down, and all around. Then I look up again. The ceiling is low, lower than the floor above would be. I poke at it, thinking maybe it's false like the drop ceiling in the kitchen, but all I hear is squeaking and skittering as if I just interrupted someone's slumber.

Yep, rodents.

I retrace the steps Maddock and I took when I showed him the passageway. Half expecting to see our footprints, the wooden floor is streaked with dust.

"Minou, where are you?" I whisper.

Hopefully, I'm not dealing with anything larger than a mouse.

I try to picture the layout of the chateau and where I am in relation to the hidden stashing place containing the Christmas decorations. I've been back here once already but can't find a way to get to them.

From above comes a creaking sound. I go still. The hairs on the back of my neck and arms lift. I listen. I don't hear Leonie on the baby monitor and the alarm system is armed. Must be the cat.

"Just keep telling yourself that," I mutter.

Then I look up at the shadows I'm making with my light. I swallow thickly then tilt my head to the side. Huh.

Coated in cobwebs, I spot something I've never before noticed gleaming from the flashlight.

It's the handle attached to a sliding drop ladder.

I tug at it, hoping to pull it down, but it's rusted in place. Propping up my phone so I can see, I reach for the highest rung I can and then using the wall, walk myself up so I'm perched at the bottom. From my weight, the thing abruptly drops a few feet and my stomach whooshes. I let out a stifled shriek, not wanting to wake the baby.

"Sorry, sweetie. Mommy is in the wall. Don't mind me. Nothing to see here," I mutter the last part, having sworn off creeping around like this years ago, well, until Maddock came along.

It was easier to show him my old life than to tell him.

I climb the rest of the ladder and reach the rafters ... to one side is a crude plaster ramp that's the reverse of the staircase. Shining the light, I follow its glow and see that it leads to the Christmas decorations. Excitement rushes through me.

It's arduous, but I start to haul the boxes out one by one. Why on earth Eloise or Hogan did this, I may never know, but I feel like I struck gold, er, treasure. However, some of the boxes are incredibly heavy and I have to push them up the ramp.

With the last one remaining, I'm nearly done when I hear another strange sound. It's a splitting noise, kind of like ice cracking or paper ripping.

Then, with a crash, I slide down the ramp to the bottom. It broke, taking my phone with it in the debris. My backside and pride are already sore. But now it's official. I need help.

And fast because I can't have Leonie wake up and for me not to be there.

Without a ladder or something to hold on to, I can't climb out of here. I start to stack the pieces of the ramp on top of the last box, hoping I can jump up into the rafters when another sound stops me in my tracks.

The goosebumps return because there's nothing else for me to fall through ... and I'm not alone. But I don't think it's Minou or a mouse. A tingle runs up my spine.

Someone is outside.

# Chapter 18

## *Baby's First Christmas*

It's late and I'm over-caffeinated, making the last leg of the trip purely on coffee fumes. But I couldn't spend another night in a hotel between Nevada and Hogwash.

My hands shake a little from the road and excitement. The house is quiet, but light shines from the hallway. I tap the code into the alarm keypad and freshen up in one of the bathrooms on the lower level because I am ready to collapse onto the couch ... and cannot wait for Honey to find me here in the morning.

Heck, I don't even mind if the baby wakes me up crying. I just need a minute or two of shuteye.

After I turn off the light, I blink a few times. A faint glow burns from the adjacent room. Given my profession and the training I just taught on fire safety, I investigate. Chances are Honey plugged in a nightlight, but with electrical wiring in an old house like this, you can never be too careful.

Rubbing my eyes, I'm not sure what I'm seeing. If I didn't know better, I'd argue that the wall is glowing. If this place is radioactive, I'll wake the baby and get us out of here even though interrupting an infant's sleep is a big no-no according to "Babyhood."

I crouch, running my hand along the crack between the plaster and the baseboard. It's almost as if there's a light on inside the wall. From afar, I supervised the alarm system install and there haven't been any workers in the house since. Plus, I rescheduled the more intensive remodel for the new year so I could oversee it and not bother Honey.

But this is odd.

Trying to puzzle it out, I start to wonder if I'm seeing things. Sixteen hours of straight driving could be messing with my head.

Then I hear a faint noise, almost like a sneeze.

The roar of the road is in my ears, but then I hear it again.

Listening, I'm on alert. I bang on the wall. If it's a mouse, I'll be calling an exterminator first thing in the morning.

"Get out of here," I bark, banging my fist on the wall.

A scuffling sound follows and the old house creaks. Honey wasn't exaggerating when she said she'd been hearing things.

Giving my face a rub, I'm about to return to the couch—which has never looked so comfortable when I go still.

"Maddock?" a small, muted voice says.

I whip around, expecting Honey's figure to fill the doorway, but it's dark.

Concern grows over just how tired I am.

"It's me," she says.

My breath catches because now I have one of two problems on my hands. It's either my mental well-being or this house is haunted. Either way, something is wrong.

"I'm here," the voice says.

That's definitely Honey and her voice is muted, not airy like how ghosts are portrayed in the movies.

"What is going on?" I ask, not sure I want to hear the answer.

"It's me. I need your help."

She's not the only one.

I flip on another light. "Where are you?"

She clears her throat. "Um, I'm in the wall."

I squint as if I have X-ray vision. "You're where?"

"In the wall." A soft rapping comes from near the glowing light.

"What? How?" I start.

"I'll explain later, but do you remember the passageway we went through? I need you to find a rope or a ladder or something, go through there, and then you'll see a ladder fixed to the inner ceiling. Climb up and a passageway leads to where I am."

Suddenly wide awake, I have about a dozen questions, but safety first. Well, except the manner in which I'm about to do this contradicts the importance of safety and teamwork that I just taught the guys. If I somehow get trapped, it's game over. But I have my phone, it's charged, and worst-case scenario, I'll call Jesse and JQ to bring a battering ram and break us out.

Ten minutes later, a very dusty Honey is crawling into my arms. Just to annoy her, I fling her over my shoulder, fireman carry style. Only, this time, she doesn't protest.

When I set her down, her eyes are wide and filled with relief. She grips my jaw in her hands, gaze searching my face. "What are you doing here?"

"Rescuing you, obviously. Anyway, I'm the one with the questions." I point to the wall and my mouth opens and closes like a goldfish.

The seriousness in our expressions dissolves and we both try to suppress our smiles. I can't be mad, not even fake-mad. I wrap my arms around this woman and hug her with everything I've got. She squeezes back. All legs, wearing one of my T-shirts, she practically climbs up me like she never plans to let go. I really, truly don't want her to.

I bury my head in her honeysuckle-scented hair, breathing deeply, fully, finally home.

We both pull back, eyes meeting for a long moment. Hers get heavy and flit to my lips. I dip my mouth toward hers. We connect with a brief kiss because we both have explaining to do.

After Honey tells me about finding the ancient boxes of Christmas decorations, discovering her in the wall makes slightly more sense. Still, it's rather perplexing.

"Why didn't you tell me you were coming tonight? I would've—" she starts.

"I pulled into the parking lot at a motel but couldn't get out of the truck. Missed my girls too much. Figured I'd press on until I couldn't. Didn't want to get your hopes up in case I hit New Orleans and had to pull over and sleep. Better to get here whole than wind up a pancake on the interstate."

Her lips twist with a smile. "What makes you think you'd get my hopes up, Hotcakes?"

I sling my arm around her waist, lassoing her into my lap. She doesn't resist the landing. My inhale flares when she smirks at me and sinks into my arms.

"Hotcakes, I like that, Hotcakes," I say, calling her by the same.

Can we share a nickname? Yes, we can and we will.

Resting her head on my shoulder, Honey says, "When you first got to town, everyone at the restaurant was speculating about a firefighter who saves people and houses. We agreed that Hogwash needed saving, but I asked myself if I did. Turns out, yes. I needed to be saved from my hardheaded, stubborn self who refused to ask for help."

"Honey, you did the heavy lifting."

"Let's call it a group effort." She lets out a sleepy sigh.

"By the way, rescuing someone from inside a wall was a first."

However, I can't help but think about how, in so many ways, she rescued me, from limping down a long road of bitterness and loneliness. I'd pledged never to date again, and definitely not fall in love. I was on a path of destruction, ready to level Hogwash.

Instead, I found a second-chance family.

I say, "My Captain and longtime friend recently told me that I have a habit of rushing into things."

"That probably helps when it comes to burning buildings."

I think about Captain Leyton's instructions to *Stop, Assess, Act.* This woman makes my pulse explode, but I don't want things to blow up as they did last time. "But that didn't help in my previous marriage. I know better than to rush this between you and me, but I do want there to be a you and me. I don't want to push you too hard, too fast."

She laughs a smoky laugh. "You do realize you're speaking to the driver of a Porsche."

"It's been noted. So does that mean what I think it means?"

"Real talk on babies."

I wink. "I've become sensitized."

She laughs. "You mean you're cured? No longer allergic? You have a beating heart in your chest like a real human being and not a beast?" She presses her palm to my chest.

I laugh and plant my hand on top of hers, lacing our fingers together.

"What changed?" she asks.

My gaze drifts to Honey and then the baby monitor where Leonie sleeps peacefully. "I don't know, but I remember the exact moment when it did. It was the first time I looked into Leonie's eyes. As a kid, I never thought much about being a dad. Didn't have a sister or ever play house. My Dad beat prostate cancer before I was born. After, it returned, I was told I was at high risk and might never be able to have kids. I shoved the whole notion out of my mind. Developed an aversion, I suppose."

She nods in understanding. "Maybe you did that to protect yourself. If you tell yourself you don't want something, you won't be disappointed when you don't get it."

I snort. How right she is. "Exactly."

"I'm all too familiar with that line of thinking. Cory and I had something special and—" She goes quiet as if she still holds a candle for him.

My shoulders drop because the affection in her voice makes me worry that I'll never measure up.

She continues, "When he joined the military, we agreed to go our separate ways. I didn't want to wait around for him. It was stupid, but I haven't always been known for my bright ideas or for driving in the slow lane. He had a bad heart—the actual organ. Not his kindness, generosity, or friendship. I've always wondered what our future would have been had he made it back and found me waiting. But it was too late. Our relationship had an expiration date."

The sadness in Honey's voice is painful. I want to heal the ache.

She clings to me and then looks up with a smile on her face. "I'm not going to let someone as hot as you get away this time."

Her comment tells me she's okay ... and something else very important. "So, you think I'm hot?"

She fans herself. "Hotcakes."

I say, "I've been taking ice baths because when I think about you ..."

"You haven't even lived through a Louisiana summer yet. You haven't experienced *hot*."

"Not *yet*. But it's you that sets me ablaze with that sassy mouth, your wise eyes, and just enough swagger not to put up with my ego."

Our mutual laughter shifts into a contagious yawn as the big grandfather clock chimes with the late hour.

"Leonie is going to be hungry soon."

"Then we should get some shuteye," I say, mine drooping.

Head lolling, she nods like she's about to doze off. I slide my arm under her legs and scoop her up, bring her upstairs, and say goodnight.

Nestled in the Pack 'n Play, Leonie slept through all the excitement. But now that I'm home, the excitement is just beginning.

Even though I want nothing more than to go to sleep, the wall is still glowing. I grab some safety gear from my truck and retrieve Honey's phone, turn off the flashlight, and grab the final box because I know that if I don't do this now, she'll ask tomorrow.

On Christmas, I wake up to the smell of pancakes and the sound of singing.

Merry Christmas to me. This is the best gift I could've gotten and I'm glad I pushed through the long drive last night, and not only because Honey would've been trapped in the wall.

"Good morning!" she calls when I stagger into the kitchen.

Leonie roars and lunges toward me from her high chair.

"My beauties. Also, this is new." I gesture to the high chair.

"Mara got a replacement and gave me this one."

"How generous."

"I'm trying to be the opposite," Honey says.

I tuck my chin. "Greedy?"

"No, the opposite of how I was and accept people's generosity."

"Which reminds me, on Christmas, is it better to give or receive?" I ask.

She arches an eyebrow. "Is this a trick question?"

"No, it was a discussion the guys and I were having."

"Is it a trap?" Honey asks.

"No, but speaking of trapped, just last night, you were trapped in the wall. Have you looked through your loot yet?"

She laughs. "Lots of vintage Christmas decorations, including a little wooden village kind of like the ceramic one Betsy has at the salon, but the buildings are miniatures of some here in town. It has to be one of a kind. I just can't fathom why they were hidden away."

"And I can't fathom why I haven't dug into breakfast yet. It smells amazing."

She dishes me up a plate. "Presenting, flapjacks."

I look up sharply, wondering just how much she's changed because, truth be told, I liked Honey the way she was. More than liked ... "You mean pancakes?"

"Officially, the recipe says they're flapjacks." She reminds me about the cookbook she found that belonged to Eloise Tickle.

I take a hearty bite. "They're delicious. Like a mouth hug."

"And there I thought I was the *pancake* queen."

I hug her waist. "You're my queen whether you make pancakes or flapjacks."

She tips her head back with laughter. Gone is the uptight, tense woman who argued with me about flapjacks and Hugwash. I'll give her credit for setting me straight and I'll take an equal portion for setting her at ease. She's not alone. She can trust me. I care about her more than I've done anyone and nothing is going to change that.

I ask, "Speaking of food, what's on our Christmas meal menu? We can head to the market later before they close."

"Since this is our first Christmas in the chateau, we could make Eloise's traditional meal." She opens the cookbook and shows me recipes for roast duck, crawfish dressing, collards, and pie.

"I like that idea."

Honey frowns. "It says here Hogan loved liver pate."

I wrinkle my nose. "That idea, not so much. What kind of pie?"

"Apple."

"Now you're speaking my language." I pat my belly.

"But not Leonie's. She gets baby milk until next year," Honey says.

Which is only a week away, meaning she'll be six months old.

We focus our attention on her as we finish breakfast and I can't help but feel this is the start of a new tradition—flapjacks for Christmas breakfast and pancakes the rest of the year.

The remainder of the day is spent decorating with holiday music playing in the background. It's hard not to pause every few minutes and wonder about the relics from the Tickle's Christmas collection.

"It feels like there are stories here. Literally. Look, this must be an original copy of the Christmas Carol by Charles Dickens." Honey holds it carefully in her hands.

"Is that the one with the ghosts?"

"Past, present, and yet to come."

I rather like the notion of a future with Honey and Leonie. A smile makes my eyes crinkle.

"What?" Honey asks, noticing the change in my expression.

"This is a lot different from what I was doing last year."

"Do I want to know what that was?"

"Probably not. Let's just say it involved an empty and then broken bottle of wine called Fee-fi-fo-fum or something."

"Do you mean *Fifolet?*" Honey smoothly pronounces it *fee foo lay*.

I snap my fingers. "Yeah, that's it."

"I thought you're from Nevada. That's a Cajun folklore thing. Like when you get the spirits in you—the *gris-gris.*"

"The gray gray?"

She sounds it out. "Gree gree. Kind of like dark magic. Makes people mean and is also a kind of local wine."

I shudder. My ex definitely had the *gree gree.*

Honey sticks out her tongue. "I take it you weren't the one drinking the Fifolet."

"Definitely not. But I don't want to think about that while we're celebrating."

The day is a delight with gifts exchanged—the baby loves her chirping chicken stuffed animal and Honey already wears the personalized name necklace with *Leonie* in fancy script that I had custom-made in Carson. We snuggle by the fire even though it's barely below sixty degrees. This old house is drafty, which is a problem I plan to fix in the new year.

Which comes all too soon. Honey insists we leave the decorations up for twelve more days and wants to make another special recipe from the cookbook involving black-eyed peas and cornbread.

"Have you thought more about the new menu for the Grille?" I ask.

"My goal is to get it finalized and printed before December thirty-first. That gives me plenty of time."

I chuckle. "So by the end of this upcoming new year."

She nods. "My other New Year resolution is to read my mail. All of it."

"That also gives you three hundred and sixty-four days."

She sighs. "I already got through everything except the bills and my mother's letters. I figure it's best to give myself a long runway for that."

I want to assure her that I'll help however I can but figure that's a conversation for later. After all, we have fifty-two weeks to figure things out, including whether I'm going to leave periodically to teach trainings sessions out west. But we'll get to that.

Honey's expression dims, and she says, "Maddock, there's something else ... Something I want you to know about me. Um, remember how I mentioned that my mother is in jail?"

I nod slowly, surprised that she wanted to head into this territory since it seems like a sensitive topic.

"I was born behind bars and it's like I've kept them around me even though her crimes weren't my crimes." She winces. "Though for a time, I was complicit."

Gripping Honey's shoulders, I want nothing more than to soothe this sudden sadness out of her, but before I can say anything, she continues, "My mother has been sending me letters, warning me about my cousin."

"Leonie's birth mother?"

She nods.

I tip her chin up. "Don't worry. I'm here. Nothing is going to happen. Let's make a New Year's resolution together. The ghosts of the past get left there. You and me, we're starting a new chapter, telling a new story, together."

Her smile rises to her eyes and then falls. "Ghost."

I brush my thumb by her lower lip. "And a future together yet to come."

She says, "No. I mean yes. Absolutely. But it just came to me. Finding Eloise's cookbook connected me to a time in this house before all of my mother's schemes. When the tree was aglow—"

I point to ours.

She nods. "And the stockings were hung—"

I tip my head toward the hearth.

"Exactly. But there was something about the notes in the margins of the cookbook. The ones about the apple tart and liver but not heart."

"I'm more than willing to cook anything you make ... even liver." I swallow thickly.

She laughs, almost ecstatic as she hops to her feet. "No, it's not that. The riddle on Tickle's tombstone."

I'm not sure what she's getting at as I try to recall it and swipe open my phone to the photo of the riddles and read, "'Take one from apple but none from tart. Find one in liver but not in heart. The last you'll discover in giant as well as ghost but never, ever in a roast.'"

Honey snaps her fingers, then drops to sitting. "Yes, but it still doesn't quite make sense."

"But you think the Tokens may be real?" I ask, voice full of hope. If so, I don't have to convince her and can let JQ and Lexi tell her about their discovery if they wish.

Nodding slowly, she concedes. "Given the fact that I found all those Christmas decorations behind the wall, maybe the treasures are too."

"So far, there's no gold, but—"

"But maybe we'll get lucky."

I tug Honey close and kiss her temple, "As far as I'm concerned, we already did."

She curls into me, into my lips as we move in for a kiss and the tokens and treasure hunt are forgotten for now.

My hands skim her waist and hers grip my cheeks and jaw, cementing me in place.

I'm not going anywhere. Not now. Not ever. Not with Honey in my life. My chest squeezes and my pulse goes wild just thinking about it, about us. We press together and I feel her heart throbbing, steady and true.

Her hands sweep my back and mine drop to hers as if we're glued together.

The kiss deepens and my thoughts recede. All I have, all I want, all I need is right here with this brown-eyed beauty who doesn't seem to think kissing me is gross after all.

# Chapter 19

## *Check Engine Light*

After the holidays, it's back to business as usual. Only, Maddock is looking after Leonie today. Says he's training her to be a construction supervisor as they clear the road that leads to the cemetery.

He has big plans for Hogwash and although I think most residents will take kindly, they'll also yap. Molly has no shortage of gossip to spill even though we're hardly into the new year. From the sound of it, she's seeding content for upcoming editions of the Pest Digest.

From the customer side of the counter at Laughing Gator Grille, she says, "So, are you going to enter the recipe contest at the Hogwash Hunt? Your cream brool is really good."

I want to roll my eyes but resist. Despite her "unique" personality, she has helped me out around here when I've had to take care of Leonie, and for that I'm grateful. However, I'll never let her get behind the wheel of the Porsche, which is now safely parked in the carriage house at the chateau.

I've had so much going on, there's barely been a minute for me to spare to work on the updated menu no less think about the possible connection between Eloise's cookbook and Hogan's riddle.

Molly leans in. "Keep this between you and me, but Mrs. Halfpenny was banned after she turned up to the church potluck with a pot of pork and beans with jelly beans mixed in."

"That's not so bad."

From the other end of the counter, Mr. Soto says, "There was also a marble in her meatloaf at the Church Supper last weekend—the glass kind for playing games from when I was a youngin.'"

I wince. Nothing said at this counter is just between Molly and me.

"Ooh, Don't look now, Mrs. Witt. Mr. Hotcakes and the lion cub are coming in three, two, one." Molly spins in her stool as if pleased with herself.

"My last name is Hamilton until I say otherwise." My tone is exactly what Molly would expect from me, but I rather like the way Mrs. Witt sounds. Also, how does she know about our Hotcakes nicknames for each other?

Molly rests her chin in her hand and fiddles with her sweet tea straw. "I was hoping Maddock would fall madly in love with me. Molly and Maddock have a nice ring to it, don't you think? But I'll continue to wait patiently for my Prince Charming."

Before I can respond, Leonie roars upon entry. I scoop her into my arms and play monster, gently nipping at her neck until she dissolves with laughter.

Maddock says, "Hey, that's my move."

"Sorry. Stole it."

He kisses me on the cheek and hopefully, only loud enough for me to hear, says, "That's not the only thing you stole." He pats his chest and winks.

I playfully swat him for being so cheesy, but secretly love it and he knows that.

He sits at a table with Leonie in a high chair and orders two BLTs. I don't register the double order until Antoine tosses Molly an apron.

She ties it on and says, "Lunch break. I'll take my cream brool payment when you're done."

"Did you arrange this?" I ask Maddock.

"Sure did, Mrs. Witt."

I gasp and stare at him in shock.

He takes a bite of his sandwich as if he didn't say anything unusual. Does Molly know something I don't?

I stutter, "Catch up."

He says, "Ketchup? On my fries, sure."

"I mean catch me up on what's going on," I say, popping one into my mouth.

"Oh, when I asked Molly to start covering your lunches so you could eat, she wanted a scoop. Asked if you're the future Mrs. Witt."

"Despite, um, the easing of my stubborn independence, I do have a say in that."

He smiles. "Of course. Also, there've been some developments adjacent to Shady Lane."

"Do you mean like the construction of a housing development?" I'm not sure what to think of that. I like our rural plot.

He shakes his head. "The bulldozer driver found an old car parked there. Looks like someone is living in it."

From two booths over, Jesse cranes his head and says, "It's not Sawyer. He's staying with Thelma at the Pigs in a Blanket for the time being. Speaking of Mrs.—"

Molly appears like a ghost and asks, "What do you know? Is Sawyer going to propose to Roxy?" she squeals.

Leonie does, too.

I mutter, "Nothing is private in this place, I swear."

"Any idea whose car?" I ask Jesse.

"Ran the plates. Stolen vehicle out of New Orleans. Trunk full of empty bottles of Fifolet."

"Figures." Probably the first of the scavengers for the hunt. Even though it's waned in popularity in recent years, people still turn up.

"No one is going to be dumping their trash—found some of that—oyster shells, or stolen vehicles down that way anymore," Maddock says with finality.

Leonie claps like she seconds that motion. But something about the car bothers me and not just because we may have a petty criminal on our property. However, I can't put my finger on what it is.

That evening, after dinner, we take a walk down the newly widened lane that passes the cemetery and leads to the Metairie Stronghold. The sweeping live oaks covering the road were enchanting but the lower limbs and older growth posed a hazard, so now it's a bit clearer and brighter.

Maddock points to a spot toward the swamp. Minou sits on a rock, licking her paw. "Jesse had that car towed out of here."

"Good riddance. I wonder if that's what I was hearing while you were gone."

"Could be." We pass the graveyard and he wiggles his fingers. "Or ghosts, zombies, or the crocogator."

I poke him in the ribs. "Don't even try to use my devilry against me."

We both laugh, Leonie too, even though she has no idea what we're talking about.

Maddock outlines his plans for the area, and I'm warming

to the idea because it'll also mean more business for the Laughing Gator Grille.

When we get back to the house, the sun has sunk behind the trees, casting shadows all around. To an outsider, this might seem a spooky scene, but it's much improved from years past.

However, I startle when I spot someone sitting on the porch steps that lead to the kitchen. A bottle of Fifolet hangs in her hand. I let out a slow breath like a ghost is stealing it from me.

My voice rasps when I say, "What are you doing here?"

The woman on the steps eyes Maddock and chuckles. "Going after my scraps, huh?"

"What?" I ask, my voice full of venom because Ambrette is unwelcome here.

It's then I realize Maddock stopped a few steps behind me. His eyes blaze dark and forbidding.

"Hey, Macksie," she says with a nasty smirk.

He doesn't move so much as a muscle.

"Don't act like you don't know me and don't be mad."

His nostrils flare. "Emberly, I suggest you leave now."

Emberly? This is Ambrette, Queen of Hearts, Babie's daughter. My cousin.

"What are you doing with my husband?" she barks.

Two things collide inside of me. Ambrette doesn't ask about Leonie. But does she mean that Maddock is her husband? That can't be right.

Another thought nearly knocks me over. If that's the case, could Leonie be his daughter? I stagger backward as I internally freak out, wishing I hadn't let myself fall for him. This is so on brand for Ambrette to con me. First, by leaving me her child and then getting her partner in crime to fool me into thinking there's something between us. The details are different, but this certainly isn't the first time. Gritting my jaw and shaking my head, I'm just not sure how quickly I'll be able to pick myself up this time.

Maddock steadies me by gripping my elbow. "You okay?"

I jerk my arm away. "Yeah. Of course. Why wouldn't I be?"

In the past, this would've been true. I'd just breeze on by, not letting anything ruffle my feathers. But I am ruffled. Flapped. Not cool and certainly not a cucumber. If I had a baseball bat, I'd smash something.

Trying to hide the battle of emotions raging inside, I ask my cousin, "Did you want to see—?" Never mind all that, I almost can't bring myself to ask whether she wants to be part of Leonie's life.

"That's not why I'm here." She turns to Maddock. "Macksie, baby. I was wondering if you could help me out."

*Macksie?* I mouth.

Nostrils flared, he shakes his head. "I'm wondering if you can explain what is going on."

Torn between anger and confusion, I say, "I was going to say the same thing." If I were more of a hospitable southern woman, I'd invite Ambrette inside, pour us some sweet tea, and we'd discuss this—whatever it is—like civilized adults.

I know well enough that she's anything but.

A pair of headlights shine and Ambrette stiffens. The roof rack on the vehicle reveals it can only be one person. Jesse exits the police SUV. My cousin could make a run for it, but she seems frozen. Like she doesn't have anywhere to go other than the swamp—not a good idea at dusk.

"Deputy," Maddock says with a nod.

Jesse gives me a knowing look, but I'm afraid there's more to the story than delinquent teenagers growing up in a small town. "Ah, the usual suspect. Just who I was looking for."

Peeved, I throw my shoulders back. I need to take control of the situation and say, "Maddock, meet Ambrette. Would you like to introduce me to your ex-wife?"

He narrows his eyes. "Ambrette? Funny, she told me her name is Emberly Jacobi."

"Nothing funny about it. More like juicy," Molly says, exiting the cruiser.

Jesse wears an apologetic expression. "Miss Hazelwood is doing a ride-along. Came out here to check on things after finding the stolen car. Didn't think we'd walk into a domestic dispute."

If my cousin is surprised to see he's a law officer, she doesn't reveal it, but he's right about one thing. Wherever Ambrette is, comes trouble. Never fails.

She simpers a smile. "Jesse Break-the-Law-Son. On the other side of the law now, huh?"

"The right side," he says.

Maddock starts pacing. "I can't help but feel like this is some kind of small-town setup. Explain what's going on."

"It is a small town," Molly says.

"But I was hoping you were going to do the explaining." I'm not sure what to think other than Leonie is going to fuss soon ... and apparently, my mother wasn't lying. In her letters, she said that Ambrette was back in town and had pulled the con of a lifetime—she called it the Brooklyn Bridge Sale, but I'm not sure she sold anything other than a lie to Maddock. Given his surprise and the false identity my cousin gave him, the elements of her scam start to come together in my mind. I should've known, but I thought that was all behind me.

Ambrette bats her eyelashes at Maddock. "What can I say, I found myself a hot firefighter."

His jaw ticks. I bounce Leonie on my hip so she doesn't fuss, but she reaches for Maddock, her father?

Rapid fire, I ask, "Did you elope? Have a big Southern

affair? Is Leonie his?" Possibilities take share in the part of my mind that kept track of my mother's schemes.

She shakes her head once, twice, and then nods all while wearing a wicked smile.

My cousin is known for doing crazy things—not the most stable member of the family. Then again, none of them were. Mama, Ambrette, and my mother's twin sister are all on the wrong side of the law. Aunt Babie—short for Babette—committed high-class crimes while Mama preferred to keep it down home. Looks like Ambrette decided to follow in her mother's footsteps after all.

"Well, isn't this a real kick in the pants," I mutter.

Tallula pulls into the driveway and without a word, she takes Leonie and whisks her into the house. Jesse must've called backup of the non-officer kind.

Ambrette says, "I'm here because I miss you, Macksie. I thought we could try again."

He says, "The Titanic lie is sinking. There is still time to jump ship."

Hands on my hips, I say, "Y'all have about two seconds to start talking or heads are going to roll."

Maddock, mirroring my posture, says, "I was going to say the same thing."

Even though I'm stunned beyond belief, and don't know who's duping who, we remain a united front. Sort of. Jesse and Molly are also here and I sense that whatever happens, they've got my back.

Rising to her feet, my cousin rolls her fingers on the handrail and looks us both over as if assessing who's more gullible.

"Out with it, Ambrette," I say, voice low and full of warning.

"Ooh. Look who's tough now. Sweet little Honey who was

too afraid to pull off jobs, all big and bad, making threats." She snorts.

I fire back, "I wasn't afraid. What you and my mother were doing was illegal and morally bankrupt." Okay, maybe I was a little afraid ... of them.

Ambrette glances at Jesse in his sheriff's uniform. "You were just as involved. I have proof."

Our deputy sheriff coughs into his hand. "Statute of limitations."

Meanwhile, Molly scribbles down notes.

Ambrette gestures to the chateau, and then her gaze lands on Maddock. "For starters, none of this is yours."

As if already annoyed by her antics, he sighs and says, "Do tell."

She starts pacing. "It was the perfect plan. I had the documents forged. Deven Chandler Esquire isn't a real lawyer. He and I cooked up—"

"So we're living here illegally?" I panic because now I really don't have anywhere for Leonie and me to go.

Maddock's nostrils flare. "That whole story about how your great-grandfather started this town or whatever was a lie?"

"Nothing she says is true," I mutter.

Almost to himself, Maddock says, "Then I'm not the bitter heir."

"You have no claim unless you have a brother who's actually related to Tickle," Ambrette says vaguely.

"Meaning Hogan Tickle had a secret son?" I ask, the historian in me curious.

She smirks, but I can't tell if this is yet more subterfuge and intrigue—a red herring.

Scowling at Ambrette, Maddock says, "You do realize you just confessed a crime and will soon be behind bars."

Ambrette's face falls. I'm more concerned about Leonie

than her nonsense, but he's right. I used to be so used to this type of conversation, even in front of Jesse, I nearly forgot that. But there is something more pressing that I need to know.

My voice is tight when I ask, "Does this mean Maddock is Leonie's father?"

He presses his hand to his chest as if soothing an ache he hardly let himself acknowledge. "I didn't think I could have kids." With a searing look that pins Ambrette in place, Maddock asks, "Is she mine?"

She snorts. "Of course she is. We were married."

"You weren't with anyone else?"

"Not that month." A chuckle escapes that she wasn't faithful to him.

"Maddock is Leonie's father?" My breath catches in my throat.

Ambrette laughs. "That's what you named the baby?"

I scowl. "Answer me."

"Only if you race me." I realize why she's here. Never mind morally bankrupt, she's run out of treats and tricks. Broke and possibly broken. This is her last-ditch bail-out effort and I'm not going to bite. Back in the day, a race wasn't just a race, it was a wager—a way to make fast cash.

I say, "You don't even have a car."

"You know I was always faster."

Flames lick my every word when I say, "The only racing I'll be doing is chasing you out of town."

Ambrette laughs like I'm joking.

I'd finally buried my old life in the past and had hope for the new one ahead when my cousin had to come back and spook up old ghosts. With Leonie safely inside, I snap—tree limb in a storm style.

One second I'm standing outside, the next I'm behind the wheel of the Porsche and smash through the rotted wooden door of the carriage house—it needed replacing anyway, but who cares? This isn't even Maddock's property.

Jesse waves his hands as if to stop me, but his effort is feeble as if to only say he is doing his job—and halfheartedly at that. To my surprise, Molly cheers me on, but probably so she can have more content for the Pest Digest.

Ambrette shrieks as the Porsche's headlights bear down on her. She runs toward the cemetery. This isn't an all-terrain vehicle and I stop, chest heaving. My pulse knocks against my bones.

"What got into me?" I ask, eyes burning.

I'm literally chasing Ambrette in my car. This is not who I am. Could be that my personal check engine light is on.

In the rearview mirror, a figure approaches. Maddock can deal with her. This has become all too much. Just as soon as something good happened, it all came crumbling down. Story of my life. I flip around, zoom past Jesse, and down Shady Lane toward Daley's farm with its wide open golden fields that somehow make the sky seem bigger, but it's raining. The windshield blurs and not just because of the weather. Tears flow freely and I roar with frustration.

The speedometer climbs and I anticipate police flashers behind me. The rally flags at the end of the strip. Cory pumping his fist in the air. But it's just me and a few sleepy cows chewing their cud. Those days are over. The flame has gone out. I'm no longer a wild child rebelling against rebellion —of the Luckie and Ambrette variety.

I'm a mother now and while I'd like Maddock to fit into my story, it's time to let go.

Chest heaving, I catch my breath and then speed back toward town, but instead of returning to the scene of the crime, I stop in front of the clock tower where the time is right twice a day.

I wish Maddock was here. I'd text him but left my phone in the house. I'd apologize, but I didn't do anything wrong other than have a convict for a cousin, then speed off in a fit, trying to escape that part of my life. Maybe I just needed that one last burst of speed, to prove that I can't outpace my life, that like a race track, it'll just loop back around until I deal with my problems ... and I can't do that alone.

I send up a prayer. The time may not be right, but the time is now to finally let go of all those old ghosts. I see so clearly that Maddock and I were both my cousin's marks. But she didn't anticipate her scheme bringing us together. That tells me one thing. We came out on top.

"Hey," a deep, smoky male voice calls from the darkness. "I'm no sheriff, but I don't think you're supposed to park here."

I rush toward Maddock and stop short. "Where's Leonie?"

"Safe and sound with Tallula and Molly. They're making dinner."

I wince because I don't entirely trust the latter in a kitchen.

"And Ambrette?"

"You mean Emberly?"

"I wish I could've warned you." My voice sounds raw out here in the rain.

"She had a Queen of Hearts tattoo. I never said her name because I wanted to forget about her entirely, not that it would've helped. But now the connections are so clear."

"Emberly Jacobi. In the past, she also went by Tami Stefani, Jewel Ryder, and others."

"Is Honey Hamilton your real name?" he asks, gaze landing softly on me.

"On my honor."

He lets out a breath. "This changes things. We can't stay at the chateau, but we'll figure out something."

My heart beats out a little throb of fear followed by hope as I latch onto his words.

"We?" I ask tentatively.

"You, Leonie, and me."

I lift my eyes to him, searching his face. "You're her father."

"I'm not sure what to think, but the first time I saw her—"

"The eyes—" we both say at the same time.

He says, "We'll follow all the legal channels, but whatever the case, I'd like for us to be a family."

I melt inside. "The only problem with that is you're a leaper and I'm a tip-toer."

He juts his chin at the Porsche. "I find that hard to believe given the car you drive. More like a racer."

"Some people race toward. Others race away."

Maddock grips my waist. "Which way are you going, Honey?"

I take a deep breath. "Into your arms, if you'll take me."

He opens them wide. "I will."

Before I move, I say, "I'm sorry I ran off. It won't happen again."

Understanding ripples across his features. "I know."

"Thank you."

He pulls me close and says, "I'll love you forever if you let me."

I melt into him and soon our lips meet.

I'm kindling and he just set me ablaze.

Even in the rain.

Maddock's stubble gently scratches my cheeks, then my neck as he pauses and trails a kiss behind my ear, somehow knowing how that practically makes me purr. I breathe in his cedarwood and smoke scent, moving my hands up his back and looping them around his powerful shoulders to his arms that hold me steady.

Our mouths reconnect and we return to the kiss with a rhythmic give and take. Our breathing turns synchronous, our heart beats too.

Maddock's rough palms brush along my arms before he laces his hands through mine. My skin tingles and I feel him burning for me.

Nothing can extinguish the flame between us. Not even the rain. But eventually, we part, trading a knowing smile.

Yes, I want him ... to kiss him. To do life with him. He draws me under the portico of the clock tower.

He says, "With the car's headlights beaming along with the fog and rain, this feels like a scene out of *Back to the Future*."

I giggle because he's spot on. "It was my favorite movie and not because they go back in time. I don't want anything to do with that. It's because they go fast."

"At the speed of light. What's the Porsche's top speed?" he asks.

"A shade over two hundred."

He gawks. "Have you gone that fast?"

"Only on an authorized race track." Taking a deep breath, it's time to tell him my last secret. "Aside from aiding and abetting Ambrette and my mother, I wasn't entirely innocent. My tattoo is of two crossed checkered flags. I'd drag race. Then, shortly after I turned eighteen, a professional recruiter approached me one night at Farmer Daley's. We called it The Stretch because if you couldn't get your car up to top speed before the bend in the road, there'd be a bottleneck before it straightened out again and the other driver would crash and burn. It was a particularly tricky spot."

"Let me guess, you'd nail it."

I can't help my smile. "Every time."

"I'd expect no less."

"He said I had real talent. Asked me to compete. It was my dream."

"That's amazing. You were a professional race car driver? You won that trophy," he says, referring to the one at the Grille.

"Took regionals and was on my way to nationals, plus lots of smaller races in between." I shake my head slowly. "Then Cory died. A few years later, my mother was arrested. I promised myself never to scheme or swindle. When the Guidry's left me high and dry with the restaurant, it was all I had. Taking over the Grille forced my hand. I had to put my head down and focus ... give up my dream."

"On others, not on racing."

I nod. "How else was I going to get by? If I made my life small, I'd avoid tragedy."

"There's nothing small about your personality."

I snort a laugh. "I always said I'd go back to the track when ..." My voice drops to a whisper. "When the time was right."

"Twice a day." Maddock points to the clock.

A smile slowly blossoms on my lips. "I guess so."

"Now that I probably don't own this town, since Emberly, er, Ambrette forged everything, I'm not sure I'll be in the position to fix it." He takes a deep breath and adds, "But I don't want to waste another moment before telling you the truth."

My stomach leaps into my throat.

Eyes twinkling, he says, "I love you, Honey."

I expect my breath to falter, to feel twitchy inside. To want to resist. But the fight in me has left, leaving room for only one thing.

"I love you too."

We seal this moment with another kiss.

When I emerge from the fog of this man's lips on mine, I say, "Maybe there is treasure in Hogwash after all. But it isn't hidden away and buried, it's right—"

Maddock nods. Once more, our lips meet. Yes, this is the real treasure.

# Epilogue

## One Week Later

### Honey

I've just closed the Laughing Gator Grille for the day, but instead of working on the new menu (a work in progress), I pull out a lollipop and finish writing my mother a letter. I'll never forget all the trouble she caused me, but I am working on forgiving her little by little. Plus, seeing pictures of Leonie seems to brighten her days behind bars, so I agreed to send her a monthly update.

Someone raps on the door and I startle. It's Jesse looking windswept and wicked.

I open the door and let him in, concerned about what's going on. His feet are sopping wet and he's nearly out of breath.

"Came as fast as I could."

The blood rushes from my body. "Is it Leonie?"

"No, she's with Tallula."

"Is it Maddock?"

Bracing his hands on his thighs, he shakes his head. "Nope. He's, uh, busy."

I tilt my head with suspicion.

"Nothing to worry about there."

Before I can badger him into spitting it out, Molly appears with Roxanne at her heels. "Which way did it go?"

"What is going on?" I ask.

"If you'd stop peppering me with questions—" Jesse starts, sucking in a long breath.

"Can I get you some sweet tea?"

"That would be great," He doesn't move from the mat by the door.

Molly and Roxanne edge past him as if eager to get the scoop.

I hand Jesse the drink and he takes a long sip. "As you know, we've been trying to track down Ambrette since the night she appeared at the chateau then took off for points unknown."

All three of us lean in.

"I was on patrol as usual, not thinking much about that when I spotted her hauling her tin can through the swamp at top speed."

"Her tin can?" Molly asks.

"Her butt," I say, eager for Jesse to continue.

"I came to a stop and she streaked past with," he takes a big breath, "a behemoth on her tail."

"The crocogator was chasing her?" I say, barely above a whisper.

He nods.

"That's not real," Molly says.

When we're both quiet, she says, "It is?" She looks as pale as I must've been moments ago.

"Did you—?"

"I'm not sure what I could've done. That thing was moving fast. Must've been at least fourteen feet long. Maybe more."

"And albino," Roxanne adds.

He nods.

I glance at my letter on the table. "If my mother got wind, there'd be a prison break. She insisted the crocogator was real." The Tokens and treasure too. But I didn't believe it because she, of all people, would've gotten her hands on it.

He chuckles. "Let's hope not."

Pen poised above her notebook, Molly asks, "Where was this?"

He answers, "Over by Bladecrook."

"So nearly out of town." Molly taps her pen on her chin.

"Sounds like the crocogator was running Ambrette out of town," Roxanne says.

"Good riddance," I say, hoping that's the last we hear from my cousin.

Just then, Maddock enters, concern splashed across his features, likely at the Deputy Sherriff's vehicle outside.

Before he can ask questions, I say, "Everything is fine."

Jesse winces. "Not for Ambrette."

We fill him in while Molly and Roxanne slink away, likely scoping out a scoop. After Jesse leaves, I ask, "Did Ambrette really call you Macksie?"

"Unfortunately."

"Is Maddo okay?"

"That's for friends only."

"I'm your friend."

"My girlfriend ... but what would you think about fiancée?"

I beam a smile. "That sounds like it might be fun."

He winks. "Stay tuned." Lowering onto the booth where I was writing, he asks, "What are you working on?"

"A letter to my mother, but I was also going to pick a few recipes to test for the new menu. Antoine is excited. Any suggestions?"

Maddock flips through the pages and says, "I'm a big fan of the flapjacks. What's this say?"

"Eloise jotted notes in the margin, let me see." I angle the old cookbook for a better look.

"It's backward."

"I think that's because it was written on the backside and the lead from the pencil made a mark," I say, inspecting it.

I've gotten used to Eloise's handwriting and read the words on the back of the page with the apple tart recipe and recall the connection between the cookbook contents and Hogan's gravestone riddle—that got put on the back burner, so to speak, with all the drama going on recently. "'Take one from apple but none from tart.' That's part of the riddle from Tickle's gravestone."

"Why would that be in here?"

"I still haven't puzzled that out." With a shrug, I add, "Maybe Hogan left riddles for Eloise."

"In her cookbook?" He flips the pages and stops at the recipe for liver pate, then stabs the reverse side of the paper. "Look! 'Find one in liver but not in heart.'"

I tilt my head in question and we scramble to find the roast recipe. On the reverse side of the page is the last part.

Maddock reads, "'The last you'll discover in giant as well as ghost but never, ever in a roast.'"

"It makes as much sense as it ever has."

Maddock flips to a new page in my notebook where I am writing a letter to Mama. He transcribes the keywords from each of the riddles: *Apple, Tart, Liver, Heart, Ghost, and Roast.*

He doesn't move for the next three hours. Because of the legal issues related to the estate, we've been staying at Pigs in a Blanket, thanks to Thelma's hospitality, but we have dinner in the restaurant tonight because Maddock won't draw his eyes away from the paper.

But when I all but beg him to come home since it's late, he hasn't solved it.

It's not yet daybreak and Leonie is still fast asleep, a heavy thud from the bedroom upstairs wakes me up. Footfalls approach down the hall. A soft rap comes from the door.

"It's me," Maddock whispers.

"Thelma said no funny business," I whisper back through the crack in the door.

"There's nothing funny about this. I figured out the riddle. The clues had me removing letters."

"You mean you solved it?"

"One word. Very familiar. Restaurant."

"Yes, Maddock. But I don't have to be there for almost three hours. A gal needs her beauty rest."

"NO, I mean the answer to the riddle is restaurant."

I straighten. Oh. "Are you sure?"

"Positive. I tried every combination of the letters. There's no such thing as a *Raunattres* or a *Serttanuar,* at least not in English."

I laugh softly. "You are in Hogwash, but you're right about that."

"Next question, what restaurants have been here since Hogan was alive?"

"The Penny Gamble and the Laughing Gator Grille."

"Technically, the Penny Gamble is a soda fountain. Wait. Did you say the Laughing Gator Grille?"

"Yes, it had been in the Guidry family for three generations —started as a grilled gator meat shack. George and Lucille updated it, but not the menu. Which I'd like to have the energy to do today so—" A yawn finishes my sentence.

"What was it called before?"

Yawning, I say, "It used to be called *Restaurant.* The word is still painted under the alligator sign because they were too cheap to paint over it."

"Can I head over there?"

"If you promise to get me one of Lexi's Sm'ookies later."

"Of course."

I pass him the keys and go back to sleep. Hours later, I've nearly forgotten the exchange when I find Maddock inside the restaurant pacing. Thankfully, I beat the Klatch here today.

We say good morning and he asks about a dozen questions, trying to figure out why the clue pointed to *Restaurant*.

I wish I had better answers, but it's not until I'm cleaning up at the end of the day does something float into my mind. "The restaurant," I whisper. Then, more loudly, "The Christmas decorations."

Maddock's eyes grow wide as if he knows what I'm talking about.

I don't finish mopping and we race to the door and lock up. Ambrette may have swindled him out of the chateau, but he's been working with legitimate lawyers to figure out recourse. It could take a while, especially since she hinted that there might be a rightful heir, but I found the Christmas decorations and we'd like to see the chateau become a hotel, if not a historic site, so we stored everything until the case is settled. Maddock invested a lot of money in rehabilitating the building and land, so at the very least, he'd like to recoup his investment ... with interest.

We carefully unpack the boxes until we come across the little painted Christmas village made of wood. Along with the soda fountain, the theater, a few other buildings, and the clock tower, we find the restaurant. I hold it carefully in my hands and turn it over.

"It feels like the bottom slides out."

Maddock takes it and gently shifts the wood. He flips the panel over and something gleams. "Is that what I think it is?"

My smile grows. "It's small, flat, and gold."

"One of Tickle's Golden Tokens," he breathes.

I turn over the golden coin in my hand. On one is a flying pig with wings and on the other is a clock with the hands pointing to three. It's shiny and smooth like it just came from the mint or wherever eccentric old men with the last name Tickle obtain things like this.

Maddock reaches inside the little restaurant cavity. "There's also a piece of paper."

"I hope it's not another riddle," I say.

Maddock unfolds the brittle paper and reads, "'Times change. So you don't forget, find my brother under the tower at three o'clock.'"

"Times do change," I say.

"But whose brother do you think it could be?"

I shrug and rub my finger over the clock. "I'm guessing the message means the clock on the coin."

A moment that's as quick as lightning passes between us before we both utter, "Back to the Future."

Maddock and I jump to our feet. Hand in hand, we dash to the town square. It's nearly dark and we gaze up at the clock tower, circling it once, twice, and then stand under the portico where we kissed just last week.

"Back to the Future," I repeat with a laugh.

"Let's see what else Hogan has up his sleeve."

Plywood covers the door, likely to keep Jesse out, but I try to jiggle it loose. Maddock angles his head for me to move out of the way. Like a beast, he tears it off with a splintering crack.

"I'd say ladies first, but I'm not sure it's safe." Maddock takes the lead up the creaky wooden stairs.

It's slow going as we pick our way carefully. When we reach the top, I look out over Hogwash Holler, wishing it would reveal its secrets.

He says, "I don't see much other than dust and bird doo."

I wrinkle my nose. "What do you think it meant by three o'clock?"

Maddock scratches his temple. "Maybe something is hidden behind the three on the clockface or—" He points ahead of us. "Twelve." Then, to the left, and says, "Nine."

"Behind me would be six, like when the other guys on the fire crew say 'Watch your six,' meaning always look out behind you."

"Then three." I point to where it would be if we were looking at the clock face.

We peer at the brick wall on the right. Carved into the wood that braced the crossbeam for the old bell, I notice a shape and trace my finger over what looks like a rotund oval ... with legs, hooves, and wings. "Is that a pig?"

"A flying pig," Maddock says, brushing away the dirt and dust.

Thinking of the baseboard at the chateau and my discovery, I poke its plump belly with my finger but nothing happens.

Maddock traces his finger in a circle around the pig, revealing an inlaid disk. It indents like a piano key, like where the Christmas decorations were hidden in the chateau.

"I like the way you're thinking," I say.

He turns it and reveals an opening. Inside sits a vintage metal cookie tin.

I realize I'm holding my breath.

He says, "I'm guessing these are stale. But it's pretty heavy."

I brush off the lid and read the words printed on the top. "Time Capsule. Hogwash Holler 1922."

Our gazes meet at this discovery.

He says, "That's over a hundred years ago."

"Wow. Should we open it?"

"Maybe not up here." He shifts his weight and the rotten wood makes a questionable noise that suggests it would give way if we decided to jump up and down with excitement.

"Yeah, this seems dangerous."

"So is time. It can slip past without you even realizing it." He cups my cheek, gazing affectionately into my eyes.

My gaze lifts to his.

And our lips press together for a kiss that's like a treasure hunt all its own because I keep discovering new things I adore about this man.

\* \* \*

Maddock

Back at the restaurant, with the slatted blinds closed, Honey carefully picks through the contents of the metal time capsule tin while I film for posterity. There are postage stamps, theater ticket stubs, a candy bar wrapper, some sepia-toned photos of Hogwash Holler, several peacock feathers, a root beer bottle cap, a little carved wooden flying pig, newspaper clippings, and a few other items. When she reaches the bottom, she pulls out a piece of paper.

"Is it a note?" I ask.

Honey shakes her head. "It's a stock certificate."

"For livestock?"

She inhales sharply as her eyes scan the old paper before her gaze snaps to mine. "No, like the stock market. It's original shares in General Electric."

My eyes widen and a chill brushes across my skin as I read

the information. "I don't know much about the stock market, but, um, I imagine this is worth a lot of money. Like millions."

Our eyes meet once more and we leap into a hug, screaming like we just won the lottery.

When we both calm and catch our breaths, Honey says, "Do you have any idea what this means for Hogwash?"

"That it doesn't matter who owns the chateau or the town, these funds can help revitalize it." My idea to make this place a destination while also supporting commerce and the livelihood for the locals takes shape.

For the next hour, we go back and forth, speculating about how to handle this. Rightfully, Tickle's Golden Token was up for grabs and finders equals keepers, however, the time capsule is part of Hogwash Holler's history.

"I think we need to think. Like a good gumbo, we need to let the pot simmer before we make any big decisions," Honey says, biting the inner corner of her lip.

"And we should keep this to ourselves for now."

"I'm afraid Molly probably already knows about us being up in the clock tower. But you're right."

"We can share that we discovered the Golden Token and the time capsule."

"It's tempting to keep the stock certificate to ourselves."

"This was a scavenger hunt," I say.

Her expression turns thoughtful. "That's tempting, but it's also like the Christmas decorations in the wall were a time capsule of the life Hogan led with Eloise up until she died. That's kind of romantic."

"I'm guessing she really loved the holiday."

Honey nods. "If only we could get the mayor involved."

"You mean Chick Jagger?"

We both laugh and study the contents of the time capsule

for a few more minutes before heading over to Pigs in a Blanket, stock certificate safely stowed. I'm grateful Thelma is letting us stay here, but I hope to soon move to a place of our own.

Having to leave the chateau after all that work and time invested was hard, but I followed the advice of my new lawyer who has no association with Emberly, er, Ambrette. There's a chance I could regain ownership, but it'll take some time to figure out the best angle to approach the situation from a legal standpoint.

Meanwhile, I help JQ tear down his old barn to build a new one. It's dirty and sweaty work, but the time spent focused on not getting poked by a rusty nail helps me process Emberly's deception. She kept our baby from me. Given the situation, the chances of me realizing that I had a kid, were infinitesimal. Yet, it was like nothing would stop me, not even a storm or a squall of deceit would keep me from the truth, from my family.

And for that, I have a plan. A big one ... and it involves the stock certificate. I'm going to make an investment with it for our future, but not the financial kind. More like for the security Honey wants and Leonie needs.

The next weeks are a flurry of excitement about the Token and time capsule discoveries. I spend a lot of time with lawyers —real ones as I claim co-parental rights of Leonie with Honey, a case is brought against Ambrette for scamming me with her ill-gotten gains, and determining whether I own Hogwash.

It's all stressful and unsettling—lots of strings. It's the exact opposite of the life I said I was going to lead after the divorce. Yet here I am and I wouldn't have it any other way.

While I field phone calls, make sure Honey eats three square meals a day, and spend time with our daughter, I realize there are three important things that I need to make happen as soon as possible.

A sense of frantic urgency consumes me. Bright and early on Monday morning, after a breakfast of pancakes at the Laughing Gator Grille, I load Leonie into the truck.

"Where are you guys going?" Honey asks.

"It's a surprise."

She lifts her eyebrows.

I smirk. "It's going to be a day of surprises."

"Good ones I hope. I've had enough of the other kind for a lifetime."

I kiss her on the forehead. "Great ones. Promise."

"Leonie is in this too?" She wiggles the baby's toes.

I wink. "She's my number one accomplice, but she's probably still too small to be my getaway driver."

"Please don't break any laws."

"We won't."

It takes the better part of the day, which is no picnic with a baby—though I scored major points with the ladies at the car dealership and they sped things along as I made the purchase, aka surprise number one for my number one woman.

I schedule the vehicle's delivery for later today and then Leonie and I go to a jewelry store. While I browse, she makes a face. Nope. It's *the* face. The one before she's going to let one rip.

Not going to lie. I have a bit of a panicked new dad moment. Thankfully, there's a coffee shop and bakery across the street. We dash over there. I buy a muffin so I can use their facilities as a paying customer and quickly learn how to operate a changing table in a public space.

To say I have no interest in eating the muffin is an understatement. I also just lost a gallon of liquid from sweating so much.

No sooner do we go back to the jewelry store does Honey call me.

This time, my eyes widen. To Leonie, I say, "We've been caught red-handed."

She laughs like this day out with Dad is hilarious.

But I refuse to leave without an engagement ring.

"Where are you? Why is there classical music in the background?" Honey asks.

"Oh, um, I'm showing Leonie the finer things in life." It's not exactly a lie.

"Is that so?"

"Sure is. We'll be home by dinnertime."

"Are you trying to get me off the phone?" she asks.

"No, of course not."

"Well, I called because there's been a Chick Jagger sighting." She tells me how Mrs. Halfpenny said she saw him preening in her birdbath. "There was a feather that Molly positively identified as belonging to him."

I scrub my hand down my face because my sweet little ticking time bomb will probably soon need a nap, and I think this story could've waited until I got home.

Which reminds me of my final task.

I scramble to get off the phone because the day is getting away from me. Of course, Honey is suspicious, but soon, she'll know everything.

Sensing this particular jewelry store isn't where I'm supposed to be, we try another one, but I don't see a ring that has Honey's name written all over it.

"Last one, promise," I tell Leonie because I'm afraid she's going to start to fuss soon.

The salesperson asks if I need help. "Actually, yes. I'm looking for an—" But then I see a yellow stone surrounded by white diamonds set in a silver band. Pointing, I say, "That one. That's the one."

Leonie claps her hands together.

"Definitely that one," I repeat.

"Ah, the yellow diamond. It's extremely rare." I'd love to hear the salesperson's passionate spiel about the diamond color scale, but all I need to know is that our little family has sunny days ahead and they start now.

Leonie gobs onto my nose with her gummy little mouth, and I laugh. Or maybe those days already did. But it's time to get out of here after I pay, of course. I wasn't actually going to use the baby to make a getaway.

Once we're back on the road, Leonie conks out and I make a call, setting up an appointment with a realtor for her last booking of the day.

When we get back to Hogwash, I drop Leonie off with Mara for the evening. Then I meet Honey at the restaurant where she closes up. I help wipe the tables and peer out the window. But the car delivery isn't here yet.

After taking out the trash, I check the back parking lot. It still hasn't arrived.

She closes the blinds on the door and I take one last look.

"You're acting funny." She shifts uncomfortably.

"Funny like—?"

She bites her lip. "Like you keep looking over your shoulder or—"

Just then, a car honks. I startle and blurt, "I'd hoped to get one of those giant bows, but they didn't have one available."

Her forehead furrows. "What are you talking about, Maddock?"

Taking Honey's hand, I say, "Let me show you."

Outside, the driver from the dealership hands me the keys to a Porsche Cayenne, their version of an SUV. "I thought it was time for a sensible family vehicle."

Her jaw lowers, her lips part, and she inhales sharply. "Maddock, you didn't."

I pass her the keys. "I did, Hotcakes. I'm not telling you not to drive the Spyder, but Leonie likes this model better."

Honey runs her hand along the edge of the hood, admiring the vehicle, then she leaps into my arms.

Leaning back, she asks, "This is for us?"

I nod, unable to suppress my smile at the sight of hers.

"Thank you." Honey dive bombs me with a kiss, lots of kisses, right here on the street.

When we part, I say, "Hop in."

She slides into the driver's seat like a pro. "Okay, but where are we going?"

"I was thinking we could head over to the clock tower."

She points. "We could just walk there."

"Let's drive."

She laughs and puts the Porsche into gear. I get a running commentary of all the features, which suggests she's somewhat familiar with this model, considering she's a big fan of the make.

When we reach the clock tower, I glance up. It's still set to the wrong time, but we'll soon be doing something about that.

Even though I'm in the passenger seat, I get out and open Honey's door. Taking her hand, I stand in the same place we did a week ago.

She looks at me quizzically. Taking a deep breath, I say, "We got off to a stormy start, but the past doesn't matter as much as our future and I want one with you." I lower onto my knee and add, "Will you marry me, Honey?"

Her hand flies over her mouth and she says something. Her eyes shine and her head bobbles.

Concerned, I say, "Hotcakes, I can't hear you."

Taking her hand off her mouth, she says, "I was screaming. Sorry. I didn't want anyone to call the sheriff. Yes, the answer is yes, I'll marry you."

I slide the ring on her finger. Again, we hug and I spin her around.

"Okay, but I need to sit down," she says. "I can't believe—" she stares at the engagement band. "Is this where—?"

Unable to get out full sentences, I've never seen Honey so ruffled. Usually, she's the picture of composure.

"Leonie helped me narrow down the choices," I say, getting into the driver's seat.

The Porsche handles well as I drive down Main Street and onto Metairie Road.

Honey only looks up from her dual study of the ring and the interior of the car when we get to Marais Way. "What are we doing here?"

"We have an appointment," I answer, pulling through a gate in front of a house with a for sale sign.

"Here?"

"Jesse said he always figured you'd live over here in one of these bougie houses."

"Maddock, I can't—"

"If you like it—if we like it—we can and we will live here."

The realtor gives us a tour of the house, complete with a home library and we go to the back deck overlooking the waterfront.

"There's already a dock for my sailboat," I say.

"You have a sailboat?"

"I'd like to someday. What do you think?"

Honey turns in a circle, taking it all in. "I think it's amazing, but—"

"But you know the story of The Three Pigs. We need a place that the Big Bad Wolf or a Big Bad Storm can't blow down."

She smiles. "You make a good point."

I cock my head. "Glad to hear that."

"So what do you say we buy the place, get married, and have the reception in the backyard?"

"I say yes and I love you, Hotcakes." Honey squeals like she just won a beauty pageant fair and square.

But I'm the real winner here ... and soon, Hogwash Holler will be too.

# About the Author

Ellie Hall is a USA Today bestselling author. If only that meant she could wear a tiara and get away with it ;) She loves puppies, books, and the ocean. Writing sweet romance with lots of firsts and fizzy feels brings her joy. Oh, and chocolate chip cookies are her fave.

Ellie believes in dreaming big, working hard, and lazy Sunday afternoons spent with her family and dog in gratitude for God's grace.

## Let's Connect

Do you love sweet, swoony romance?
Stories with happy endings?
Falling in love?

Please subscribe to my newsletter to receive updates about my latest books, exclusive extras, deals, and other fun and sparkly things, including a FREE eBook, the *The Secret Book Boyfriend*!
Get your free copy here: www.elliehall.com 🩶

# Also by Ellie Hall

All books are clean and wholesome, Christian faith-friendly and without mature content but filled with swoony kisses and happily ever afters. Books are listed under series in recommended reading order.

-select titles available in audiobook, paperback, hardcover, and large print-

### *The Only Us Sweet Billionaire Series*

Only a Date with a Billionaire

Only a Kiss with a Billionaire

Only a Night with a Billionaire

Only Forever with a Billionaire

Only Love with a Billionaire

Only Christmas with a Billionaire

Only New Year with a Billionaire

The Only Us Sweet Billionaire series box set (books 2-5) + a bonus scene!

### *Hawkins Family Small Town Romance Series*

Second Chance in Hawk Ridge Hollow

Finding Forever in Hawk Ridge Hollow

Coming Home to Hawk Ridge Hollow

Falling in Love in Hawk Ridge Hollow

Christmas in Hawk Ridge Hollow

The Hawk Ridge Hollow Series Complete Collection Box Set (books 1-5)

## *The Blue Bay Beach Reads Romance Series*

Summer with a Marine

Summer with a Rock Star

Summer with a Billionaire

Summer with the Cowboy

Summer with the Carpenter

Summer with the Doctor

Books 1-3 Box Set

Books 4-6 Box Set

## *Ritchie Ranch Clean Cowboy Romance Series*

Rustling the Cowboy's Heart (Book 1)

Lassoing the Cowboy's Heart (Book 2)

Trusting the Cowboy's Heart (Book 3)

Kissing the Christmas Cowboy

Loving the Cowboy's Heart

Wrangling the Cowboy's Heart

Charming the Cowboy's Heart

Saving the Cowboy's Heart

Ritchie Ranch Romance Books 1-4 Box Set

## *Falling into Happily Ever After Rom Com*

An Unwanted Love Story

An Unexpected Love Story

An Unlikely Love Story

An Accidental Love Story

An Impossible Love Story

An Unconventional Christmas Love Story

### *Forever Marriage Match Romantic Comedy Series*

Dare to Love My Grumpy Boss

Dare to Love the Guy Next Door

Dare to Love My Fake Husband

Dare to Love the Guy I Hate

Dare to Love My Best Friend

### *Home Sweet Home Series*

Mr. and Mrs. Fix It Find Love

Designing Happily Ever After

The DIY Kissing Project

The True Romance Renovation: Christmas Edition

Extreme Heart Makeover

Building What's Meant to Be

### *The Costa Brothers Cozy Christmas Comfort Romance Series*

Tommy & Merry and the 12 Days of Christmas

Bruno & Gloria and the 5 Golden Rings

Luca & Ivy and the 4 Calling Birds

Gio & Joy and the 3 French Hens

Paulo & Noella and the 2 Turtle Doves

Nico & Hope and the Partridge in the Pear Tree

### *The Love List Series*

The Swoon List

The Not Love List

The Crush List

The Kiss List

The Naughty or Nice List

### *Love, Laughs & Mystery in Coco Key*

*Clean romantic comedy, family secrets, and treasure \*These books should be read in the following order:*

The Romance Situation

The Romance Fiasco

The Romance Game

The Romance Gambit

The Christmas Romance Wish

### *The Nebraska Knights Holiday Hockey Romance Series*

Stupid Cupid

Redd, Whit & Blue

The Kiss Class

Margo & the Faux Good Luck Beau

The Ex-Puck Bunny

Love at First Skate (Tie-In)

**Love in Hockey Town (Ties in to the Nebraska Knights)**

His Jersey

My Wife

Her Goal

**On the Hunt for Love**

*Sweet, Small Town & Southern*

The Grump & the Girl Next Door

The Bitter Heir & the Beauty

The Secret Son & the Sweetheart

The Ex-Best Friend & the Fake Fiancee

The Best Friend's Brother & the Brain

Don't You Forget About Tea (Tie-In)

**SoCal Summer Kisses**

We Go Together

The One I Want

Hopelessly Devoted

**Stand Alone Titles**

Happily Ever Haunted (a romcom - ghost mashup)

The Secret Book Boyfriend (small town, grumpy sunshine)

Madeleine's Mistletoe Meet Cute (small town, mistaken identity)

Visit www.elliehallauthor.com or your favorite retailer for more.

If you love my books, please leave a review on your favorite retailer's website! Thank you! 🖤 Ellie

P.S. I have a clean fantasy and paranormal romance pen name: E. Hall that you might enjoy (best read in listed order):

### *The Court of Crown and Compass Series*

Fae of Light and Shadow (prequel)

Fae of the North (book 1)

Fae of the West (book 2)

Fae of the South (book 3)

Fae of the East (book 4)

### *RIP Magic Academy Reform School Series*

Law & Disorder (book 1)

Crime & Curses (book 2)

Mayhem & Magic (book 3)

### *Shifter Diaries*

Life Fated (book 1)

Lies Tamed (book 2)

Loss Hunted (book 3)

Love United (book 4)

Made in United States
North Haven, CT
12 July 2025

70623214R00143